THE
TWELVE
DAYS
OF
DASH
AND
LiLY

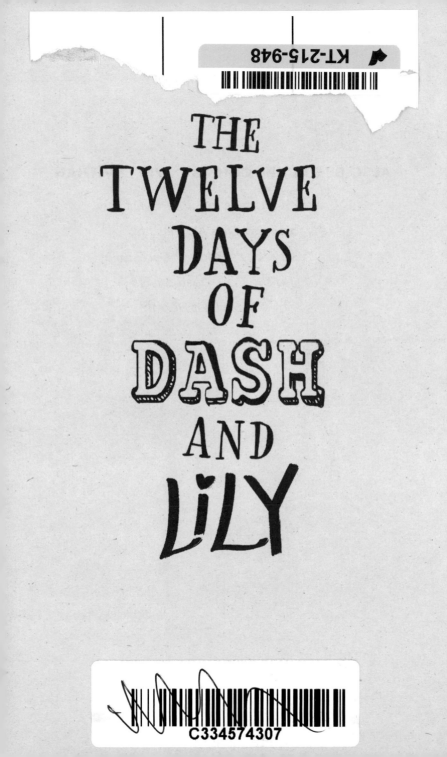

ALSO BY RACHEL COHN & DAVID LEVITHAN

Nick & Norah's Infinite Playlist

Naomi and Ely's No Kiss List

Dash & Lily's Book of Dares

Mind the Gap, Dash & Lily

Sam & Ilsa's Last Hurrah

THE TWELVE DAYS OF DASH AND LILY

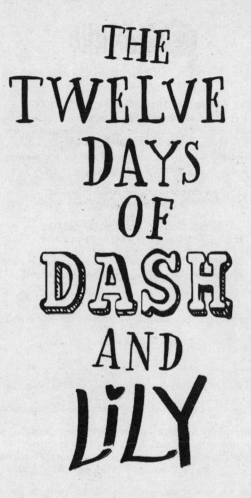

RACHEL COHN & DAVID LEVITHAN

First published in the United States in 2016
by Alfred A. Knopf, an imprint of Random House Children's Books,
a division of Penguin Random House LLC, 1745 Broadway, New York,
New York 10019, USA
First published in Great Britain in 2016 by Electric Monkey,
part of Egmont Books

An imprint of HarperCollins*Publishers*
1 London Bridge Street
London SE1 9GF

This edition published in 2020 by Electric Monkey

ISBN 978 0 7555 0006 2

A CIP catalogue record for this title is available from the British Library

egmontbooks.co.uk

64982/001

Printed and bound in Great Britain by CPI Group

Typeset by Avon DataSet Ltd, Arden Court, Alcester, Warwickshire

MIX
Paper from
responsible sources
FSC™ C007454

This book is produced from independently certified FSC™ paper
to ensure responsible forest management.

For more information visit: www.harpercollins.co.uk/green

To E.L. Konigsburg

*(for sending us on our first big
fictional adventure in NYC)*

1
DASH

A Pear in a Partridge Tree

Saturday, December 13th

I had been dating Lily for almost a year, and no matter what I did, I couldn't get her brother to like me, trust me, or think I was remotely good enough for his sister. So it was a shock when he told me he wanted to meet for lunch, just the two of us.

Are you sure you have the right number? I texted back to him.

Don't be a dick. Just show up, he replied.

The scary thing was, as much as I was trying to deny it, I knew why he wanted to meet, and what he wanted to talk about.

He wasn't right about me, but he was right that there was a problem.

It had been a hard year.

Not at the start. The start had me clutching for such plebeian terms as *awesome!* and *super!* Because Christmas

1

and the new year brought me something other than the usual consumerism and post-consumerism depression. The start of this year brought me Lily – bright, believing Lily. She was enough to get me to give credence to the notion of a benevolent fat guy in a red suit and a turbo-jacked sled. She was enough to make me feel cheer when Father Time turned over the keys to a newborn and said, *Here, drive this*. She was enough to turn me a little cynical about my own cynicism. We started the year making out in the rare-book room of the Strand, our favorite bookstore. It appeared to be an augury of good things to come.

And it was. For a time.

She met my friends. It went well.

I met many members of her seemingly infinite family. It went passably.

She met my parents and stepparents. They were confused by how their dark cloud of a son could have brought home such a sunbeam. But they weren't complaining. They were, in fact, a little in awe, to a degree that New Yorkers usually reserve for the perfect bagel, a fifty-block cab ride with no red light, and the one movie out of every five that Woody Allen aces.

I met her beloved Grandpa. He liked my handshake, and said that was all he really needed to know about me in order to approve. I sought more approval anyway, because this was a man whose eyes sparkled when he recounted a ball game played fifty years ago.

Langston, Lily's brother, needed more convincing.

Mostly, he left us alone. I didn't mind. I wasn't dating Lily to be with her brother. I was dating Lily to be with Lily.

And I *was* with Lily. We didn't go to the same school or live in the same neighborhood, so we made Manhattan our playground, gamboling through the frostbitten parks and taking refuge in Think coffee shops and every available screen at the IFC. I showed her my favorite corners of the New York Public Library. She showed me her favorite dessert at Levain . . . which was basically all of them.

Manhattan didn't mind our wanderings one bit.

January turned to February. The cold started to seep into the city's bones. Smiles were harder to come by. The snow that dazzled as it fell grew less and less welcome as it stayed. We wandered around in layers, unable to feel anything firsthand.

But Lily – Lily didn't mind. Lily was mittens and hot chocolate and snow angels that lifted from the ground and danced in the air. She said she loved winter, and I wondered if there was any season she didn't love. I worked hard to accept her enthusiasm as genuine. My mental furnace was built for immolation, not warmth. I didn't understand how she could be so happy. But such was the love I had fallen into that I decided not to question it, and to live within it.

Then.

Two days before her birthday, in May, I was asking my best friend, Boomer, for help in knitting her a red sweater. I was discovering that no matter how many YouTube videos you watch, there is no way to knit a red sweater in a single afternoon. The phone rang and I didn't hear it. Then the phone rang and my hands were occupied. It wasn't until two hours later that I saw how many messages I had.

Only when I listened did I learn that her beloved Grandpa had suffered a minor heart attack with particularly bad timing, striking as it did while he was walking up the stairs to their apartment. He fell. And fell. And lay there for at least a half hour, barely conscious, until Lily got home and found him. The ambulance took a decade of minutes to get there. As she watched, he slipped under. As she watched, they revived him. As she waited, unable to watch, he teetered, until he barely landed on the right side of living.

Her parents were in a foreign country. Langston was in class, where he wasn't allowed to look at his phone. I was too busy knitting her surprise present to notice she was calling. She was alone in the waiting room of New York-Presbyterian, about to lose something she'd never even begun to consider that she'd one day lose.

Grandpa lived, but it took him a very long time to recover. He lived, but many of the steps were painful. He lived because she helped him live, and that helping took its toll. To have him die would have been awful, but to see him continually suffer, continually frustrated, was almost as bad.

Her parents came home. Langston offered to take time off from college. I tried to be there. But this was hers. Grandpa was her responsibility; she wouldn't have it any other way. And he was in too much pain to argue. I couldn't even say I blamed him – of any of us, she's the one I'd want to be the one to help me walk again. She's the one I'd want to lead me back into life. Even if life did not feel, to her, as full of splendor as it had before.

It's always the ones who believe who are hurt the most when things go wrong. She didn't want to talk about it, and I didn't have the vocabulary to make her see it differently. She said she wanted me to be the place she escaped to, and I was flattered by that. I was supportive, but it was the passive support of a chair or a pillar, not the active support of a human being holding another human being upright. As her grandfather was in and out of hospitals for operations and complications from operations, in and out of physical therapy, she and I spent less time with each other – less time wandering the city, less time wandering the corners of each other's thoughts.

Exam time passed in a blink – then came summer. She got a job as a volunteer at the rehabilitation clinic her grandfather was going to, just to be with him more, and to help other people who needed it like he did. I felt guilty because I spent the same period shuttling between vacations with my respective parents, my father trying to outdo my mother's Montreal trip with an ill-begotten jaunt to Paris. I wanted to yell at my father for taking me to Paris, then realized what a brat I sounded like, yelling at my father for taking me to Paris. Mostly, I wanted to be away from him, and home with Lily.

Things were better with the new school year. Grandpa was walking again, was starting to shoo Lily away for her own good. I thought she'd be relieved. She acted like she was relieved, but there was still a part of her that was afraid. But instead of questioning it, I went along, thinking if we pretended all was well, there would come a moment when it would switch the groove from being a half lie to being a more-than-half truth, and then ultimately it would be the whole truth.

It was easy to think that we were back to normal, with school in full swing and all of our friends around. We had plenty of good times, able to wander the city and forget the city at the same time. There were places within her I wasn't reaching, but there were plenty of other places I could reach. The part of her that laughed at the way certain dog owners looked like their dogs. The part of her that cried at TV shows where restaurants were brought back from the brink of being condemned. The part of her that kept a bag of vegan marshmallows in her room for whenever I came over, just because I once told her how much I liked them.

It was only when Christmas came closer that the cracks began to show.

It used to be that the Christmas season would shrink my heart to the size and substance of a gift card. I hated the way the streets would clog with a thrombosis of tourists, and how the normal thrum of the city would be drowned out by tinny cliché sentiments. Most people counted down the days till Christmas in order to get their shopping done; I counted them down in order to get Christmas over with, and for the bleaker, more genuine winter to begin.

There'd been no room in my toy-soldier heart for Lily, but she'd forced herself in anyway. And she'd brought Christmas with her.

Now, don't get me wrong – it still struck me as pretty bogus to pay lip service to generosity at the end of every year only to go all generosity-amnesiac once the calendar page turned. The reason Lily wore it well was because she wore her kindness all year round. And now I was able to see it in other people too – as I sat waiting for Langston at Le Pain Quotidien, I saw this perpetual generosity in the way some of the couples looked at each other, and a lot in the way that most of the parents (even the exasperated ones) looked at their children. I saw pieces of Lily everywhere now. I'd just seen fewer of them in Lily lately.

Clearly I wasn't the only one, because the moment Langston sat down, he said, "Look, the last thing I particularly want to do is break bread with you, but we've got to do something, and we've got to do something right away."

"What's happened?" I asked.

"There are twelve days left until Christmas, right?"

I nodded. It was, indeed, the thirteenth of December.

"Well, with twelve days left until Christmas, there is a big gaping hole in our apartment. You know why?"

"Termites?"

"Shut up. The reason there's a big gaping hole in our apartment is because *we don't have a Christmas tree.* Lily usually can't wait until Thanksgiving leftovers are through before running out and getting a tree – she feels that in this city, all the good ones are taken early, and the longer you wait, the more likely you are to get a tree that isn't worthy of Christmas. So the tree is up before the first of December, and then she spends the next two weeks decorating. On the fourteenth, our family has a big tree-lighting ceremony – Lily acts like it's an age-old family tradition, but the truth is, she started it when she was seven years old, and now it just *feels* like an age-old family tradition. Only this year – nothing. No tree. All the decorations are still in boxes. And the tree lighting is supposed to be tomorrow. Mrs. Basil E. has already ordered the catering – and I don't know how to tell her that there isn't a tree to light."

I understood his fear. The minute their great-aunt – who we all called Mrs. Basil E. – opened the door to their apartment, she'd be able to smell the lack of a tree, and would not hide her displeasure at the breach.

"So why don't you just get a tree?" I asked.

Langston actually smacked his forehead in amazement at my daftness. "Because that's Lily's job! That's what Lily loves to do! And if we get it without her, it's like we're pointing out that she hasn't done it, and that will only make her feel worse."

"True true true," I said.

The waitress came, and we ordered pastries – I think we both knew we didn't have enough conversation within us to sustain a proper meal.

Once we'd ordered, I continued. "Have you asked her about the tree? I mean, about getting one?"

"I tried," Langston said. "Point blank – 'Hey, why don't we get a tree?' And do you know what her response was? 'I'm just not feeling it right now.'"

"That doesn't sound like Lily at all."

"I know! So I figured desperate times called for desperate measures. Which is why I texted you."

"But what can I do?"

"Has she talked to you about it at all?"

Even in our conversational détente, I didn't want Langston to know the whole truth – that Lily and I hadn't talked about very much in the weeks since Thanksgiving. Every now and then we'd go to a museum or get dinner. Every now and then we'd kiss, or lightly make out – but nothing that would be out of place on CBS. Ostensibly, we were still dating. But the dating was feeling rather ostensible.

I didn't tell this to Langston because I was embarrassed that I'd let it happen. And I didn't tell this to Langston because I was worried it would alarm him. My own alarms were the ones that should've been going off.

So instead of getting into it, I said, "No, we haven't talked about the tree."

"And she didn't invite you to the tree-lighting ceremony?"

I shook my head. "This is the first I'm hearing of it."

"I thought so. I think the only people who are planning to come are the family members who come every year.

Usually Lily hands out invitations. But I guess she just wasn't feeling that either."

"Clearly we have to do something."

"Yes, but what? It really feels like it would be a betrayal if I went out and bought a tree."

I thought about it for a moment, and something came to me.

"But what if there's a loophole?" I asked.

Langston cocked his head, looked at me. "I'm listening."

"What if *I* got her the tree? As a present. Part of my Christmas present to her. She doesn't know that I know about your family tradition. I could just bluster and bluff my way into it."

Langston didn't want to like the idea, because it would mean liking me, at least for a minute. But his eyes kicked in with a gleam that, for a moment, countered his doubt.

"We could tell her it's for the twelve days of Christmas," he said. "To celebrate the kickoff."

"Don't the twelve days of Christmas come *after* Christmas?"

Langston brushed this away. "Technicality."

I wasn't sure it was that simple, but it was worth a shot.

"Okay," I said. "I'll bring the tree. You act surprised. This conversation never happened. Right?"

"Right." Our pastries arrived and we dug in. About seventy seconds later, we were done. Langston reached for his wallet – I figured to pay the bill. But then he was trying to slide a few twenties my way.

"I don't want your filthy lucre!" I exclaimed. Perhaps too loudly for a restaurant of such quotidian pain.

"Excuse me?"

"I'll take care of it," I translated, sliding his money back to him.

"But you do understand – it has to be a nice tree. The best tree."

"Don't worry," I assured him, and then employed a sentence that has been the coin and currency of New York since the days of yore: "I know a guy."

It was nearly impossible for New Yorkers to get to trees, so every December, the trees came to the New Yorkers. Bodegas that were normally fronted by buckets of flowers were suddenly overrun by groves of leaning pines. Empty lots were planted with rootless trees; some establishments stayed open until the wee hours of the morning, just in case two a.m. was the time you were struck with the need to find the Xmas to mark your spot.

Some of these pop-up firriers were manned by guys who looked like they'd taken a break from drug dealing to try another kind of needle exchange. Others were staffed by guys in flannel who looked like it was the first time they'd ever left upstate and, gosh, was it big in the big city! Often they were helped out by students in need of the most temporary of temporary jobs. This year, one of those students was my best friend, Boomer.

There was, to be sure, a learning curve for him once

he started this employment. Too many viewings of *A Charlie Brown Christmas* had led him to believe that it was the most wan and wayward of shrubs that was the most desirable one, because tending to it was much more in the Christmas spirit than bringing home a self-sufficient, virulent pine. He also thought Christmas trees could be replanted once Christmas was over. That was a hard conversation to have.

Luckily, what Boomer lacked in clarity he made up for in sincerity, so the stand he was working at, on Twenty-Second Street, had become word-of-mouth popular, with Boomer as the foremost tree elf. I think this recognition was enough to make him happy he'd forsaken boarding school in his senior year to be in Manhattan. He'd already helped me pick out trees for my mother's and my father's apartments. (My mother got the much nicer tree.) I was sure he'd love the assignment of picking out the best tree for Lily. And yet I was hesitant as I got closer. Not because of Boomer . . . but because of Sofia.

Along with Boomer's jumping off board his boarding school, the new school year had brought a few surprises with it. Somewhat surprising was that my ex-girlfriend Sofia's family had moved back to New York after swearing they'd never leave Barcelona again. Not at all surprising was the fact that while I was happy to see her, it was not in a my-ex-is-back-and-there's-gonna-be-trouble way – we'd pretty much sorted that out the last time she'd visited. But it was SUPER SURPRISING when she started hanging out with Boomer . . . and hanging out with Boomer some more . . . and hanging out with him even more, so that before I could even wrap my head around the possibility, they were *a thing*. This was, in my mind, like taking the most expensive, finest cheese in the world and then melting it on a burger. I loved them both, in different ways, and seeing them together made my head hurt.

The last thing I wanted was to pop by Boomer's workplace and find that Sofia was stopping by at the same time, so they could radiate their dating vibes throughout the greater metropolitan area. They were in their honeymoon period, and that made it awkward for those of us who'd left the honeymoon behind and had entered the part of the relationship where the moon waxes and wanes.

So it was with some relief that I found Boomer not with Sofia but with a family of seven, or eight, or nine – it was hard to tell, since the kids were running around so fast.

"*This* is the tree that was meant just for you," he was telling the parents, as if he were some amazing tree whisperer and this tree had told him itself that their dining room was where it had always wanted to be.

"It's so big," the mom said. Probably imagining the pine-needle fallout all over her floor.

"It's a big-hearted tree, yes," Boomer replied. "But that's why you're feeling such a connection to it."

"It's strange," the dad said, "because I really am."

The sale was completed. As he was swiping their credit card, Boomer spotted me and waved me over. I waited until the family was gone, mostly because I was afraid of stepping on one of the children.

"Man, you really got them pining," I observed once I got to him.

Boomer looked confused. "Is that a Chris Pine reference? He is a handsome man, for sure, but I don't think any of them looked like him."

"Pine. Like tree."

"Oh! Like Chris Pine playing a tree! That would be *cool*. He's already so wooden! But not in a bad way!"

To Boomer, this thought process didn't seem circuitous at all. Which was partly why I wondered how someone as direct as Sofia could be spending so much time with him.

"I need a tree for Lily. A really special tree."

"You're getting Lily a tree?"

"Yup. As a present."

"I love that! Where are you getting it?"

"I was thinking here?"

"Oh yeah! Good idea!"

He started to look around, and as he did, he muttered something that sounded suspiciously like *Oscar Oscar Oscar.*

"Is Oscar one of your co-workers?" I asked.

"Do trees count as co-workers? I mean, they are with me all day long . . . and we have the most interesting conversations . . ."

"Oscar is one of the trees?"

"He's the perfect tree."

"Do all the trees have names?"

"Only the ones that share them with me. I mean, you can't just *ask*. That would be invasive."

He shoved aside at least a dozen trees to get to Oscar. And when he pulled Oscar out, he – *it* – looked like any other tree to me.

"This is it?" I asked.

"Wait for it, wait for it . . ."

Boomer lugged the tree away from its cohorts, toward the curb. The tree was easily a few feet taller than he was, but he carried it like it was no heavier than a magic wand. With a strange delicacy, he set it into a tree stand, and as soon as it was settled in, something happened – Oscar opened his arms and beckoned me under the streetlamp light.

Boomer was right. This was the tree.

"I'll take it," I said.

"Cool," Boomer replied. "Do you want me to wrap it? Since it's a gift?"

I assured him that a ribbon would suffice.

Catching a cab when you're a teenage boy is hard enough. Catching a cab with a Christmas tree in tow is nigh impossible. So I ran some errands until Boomer's shift was done, and together we wheeled Oscar over to Lily's apartment in the East Village.

I hadn't been there all that often in the past year. Lily said it was so her grandfather wouldn't be bothered, but I thought it was more because I'd be adding one more element to the chaos. Her parents had been around more than they'd been in years – which should have helped her out immeasurably, but instead seemed to have given her two more people to take care of.

It was Langston who opened the door, and the minute he saw me and Boomer with the tree, he said, "Whoa! Whoa! WHOA!" so loudly that I thought Lily had to be home and within hearing distance. But then he told me she and Grandpa were out at a checkup. His parents were out because it was a Saturday, and why would such social people be home on a Saturday? So it was just the three of us . . . and Oscar.

As we set him up on his perch in the living room, I tried not to notice how under the weather the apartment appeared, as if it had spent the last month or so coughing up dust and discolor. I knew the way this family worked, and I knew this meant Grandpa had been out of commission and Lily had been distracted. They'd always been the true guardians of the place.

Once Oscar was standing proudly, I reached into my backpack for the pièce de résistance that would, I hoped, not be resisted.

"What are you doing?" Langston asked as I looped things around Oscar's branches.

"Are those tiny turkeys?" Boomer chimed in. "Is this going to be like the tree they had at Plymouth Rock?"

"They're partridges," I explained, holding up a piece of wood carved in the shape of the bird, with a big hole

16

in the center. "Partridge napkin rings, specifically. There weren't any partridge ornaments at that store whose name I can't make myself utter." (The store was called Christmas Memories, which was enough to make me want to drink Pop Rocks with Coke. I had to think of it as Christmas Mammaries in order to go inside.) "If we're doing twelve days of Christmas, we've gotta do twelve days of Christmas. Lily can decorate the rest of the tree. But this is going to be a partridge tree. And on top, we're going to have . . . a pear!"

I pulled said fruit out of my bag, expecting admiration. But the reaction went more pear-shaped.

"You can't put a pear at the top of a tree," Langston said. "It will look dumb. And it will rot after a day or two."

"But it's a pear! In a partridge tree!" I argued.

"I get it," Langston said. Meanwhile, Boomer guffawed. He hadn't gotten it.

"Do you have a better idea?" I challenged.

Langston thought for a moment, and then said, "Yes." He walked over to a small photograph hanging on the wall and took it down. "This."

He showed me the picture. Even though it had to be over half a century old, I instantly recognized Grandpa.

"Is that your grandmother with him?"

"Yup. Love of his life. They were quite *a pair.*"

A pair on a partridge tree. Perfect.

It took us a few tries to get it placed – me and Langston trying out various branches, Boomer telling Oscar to stay still. But we got the pair perched near the crown of the tree as birds peeked out below.

Five minutes later, the front door opened and Lily and Grandpa returned. Even though I'd only known him a few months before he had his fall, it was still surprising to me to see how small Lily's grandfather had become – like instead of going off to hospitals and rehabilitation centers, he'd really been put in the wash for way too long, coming back even more shrunk each time.

Still, there was the handshake. The minute he saw me, he extended his hand and asked, "How's the life, Dash?" And when he shook, he shook hard.

Lily didn't ask me what I was doing there, but the question was certainly in her tired eyes.

"How was the doctor?" Langston asked.

"Much better company than the undertaker!" Grandpa replied. Not the first time I'd heard him use this joke, which meant it was probably the two hundredth time Lily had endured it.

"Does the undertaker have bad breath?" Boomer barged into the hallway and asked.

"Boomer!" Lily said. Now she was definitely confused. "What are you doing here?"

It was Langston who cut in. "Much to my surprise, your Romeo here has brought us a rather early Christmas gift."

"Here," I said, taking Lily's hand. "Close your eyes. Let me show you."

Lily's grip was not like her grandfather's. Before, our hands used to pulse electric together. Now it was more like static. Pleasant, but light.

She closed her eyes, though. And when we got into the living room and I told her to open them, she did.

"Meet Oscar," I said. "He's your present for the first day of Christmas."

"It's a pair in a partridge tree!" Boomer yelled out.

Lily took it in. She looked surprised. Or maybe the stillness of her reaction was further tiredness. Then something kicked in, and she smiled.

"You really didn't have to . . ." she began.

"I wanted to!" I said quickly. "I really, really wanted to!"

"But where's the pair?" Grandpa asked. Then he saw the photograph. His eyes welled up. "Oh. I see. There we are."

Lily saw it, too, and if her eyes welled up, they welled inward. I honestly had no idea what was going on in her head. I shot a look at Langston, who was studying her just as hard, without getting any ready answers.

"Happy first day of Christmas," I said.

She shook her head. "The first day of Christmas is Christmas," she whispered.

"Not this year," I said. "Not for us."

Langston said it was time to retrieve the ornaments. Boomer volunteered at the same time Grandpa made a move to get some of the boxes. This snapped Lily back to attention – she shuffled him over to the couch in the living room, and said he could oversee them this year. I could tell Grandpa didn't like this, but that he also knew it would hurt Lily's feelings if he put up too much of a fight. So he sat down. For her.

As soon as the boxes were brought in, I knew it was time for me to leave. This was a family tradition, and if I stayed and pretended I was family, I would feel every ounce of the pretending, in the same way that I could feel the weight of Lily pretending to be happy, pretending to want to do what we were encouraging her to do. She would do this for Langston and her Grandpa and her parents whenever they got back. If I stayed, she would even do it for me. But I wanted her to want to do it for herself. I wanted her to feel all that Christmas wonder she felt last year at this time. But that was going to take more than a perfect tree. It might just take a miracle.

Twelve days.

We had twelve days.

I'd spent my whole life avoiding Christmas. But not this year. No, this year what I wanted most this season was for Lily to be happy again.

2
LILY

Two Turtledoves
(on a Regifted Sweater)

Saturday, December 13th

I'm mad at global warming for all the obvious reasons, but mostly I'm mad at it for ruining Christmas. This time of year is supposed to be about teeth-chattering, cold weather that necessitates coats, scarves, and mittens. Outside, there should be see-your-breath air that offers the promise of sidewalks covered in snow, while inside, families drink hot chocolate by a roaring fire, huddled close together with their pets to keep warm. There is no better precursor to Christmas than a quality goose bump chill. It's what I count on to usher in the good cheer, happy songs, excessive cookie baking, favorite-people togetherness, and the all-important presents of the season. The days before Christmas are not supposed to be like this one was, a balmy seventy degrees, with holiday shoppers wearing shorts and drinking iced peppermint lattes (yuck), and tank-top-wearing Frisbee players nearly giving concussions to dogwalkers in Tompkins Square Park with their carefree spring-day bad aim. This year the cold couldn't be bothered to bring in Christmas, so until it could, I wouldn't bother getting too excited about the best time of the year.

There wasn't enough cold outside, so instead I brought it inside and turned it on Dash, who didn't deserve it.

"If you have to go, then go," I said brusquely. *Brusque*. It was such a Dash word – obscure, unknowable, distant – that it felt strange I even knew it. Along with the other million obligations overwhelming me at the moment, there was SAT study time, which left an *amaroidal* taste in my mouth. (How could an SAT taker possibly be more prepared for university by knowing such a word? Right – not at all. Complete waste of word, complete waste of time, complete certainty I will still not achieve my parents' hopes for my college admissions prospects by the addition of the word *amaroidal* to my vocabulary.)

"You don't want me to stay, do you?" asked Dash, as if he was pleading for me not to demand his spending any additional time with my beleaguered Grandpa and my brother, who at best tolerates my boyfriend and at worst is downright rude to him. I'd feel bad about Langston and Dash's animosity except it seems to be an enjoyable sport between them. If Lily was the subject on *Jeopardy!*, the answer would be, "She does not understand it *at all*," and the question would be, "What is the human male species?"

"I want you to do what you want to do," I responded, but what I meant was: *Stay, Dash. Please. This Christmas tree gift is so lovely and exactly what I didn't know I needed*

– for the season, and from you. And even though I have a ton of other things I need to do right now, there's nothing I want more than for you to decorate the tree with me. Or for you to sit on the sofa and watch me bedazzle it while you make snarky comments about pagan traditions misappropriated by Christianity. Just to have you near.

"Do you like the tree?" Dash asked, but he was already buttoning his pea coat, which was too heavy for such a warm day, and looking at his phone like there were text messages on it beckoning him to better places than at home with me.

"Why wouldn't I?" I said, not willing to further profess my profuse thanks. I had only just started sorting through the decorations when Dash announced his intention to leave, and he did it at the exact moment that I opened the gift box from the Strand that Dash had given me last January 19, to celebrate author Patricia Highsmith's birthday. Inside the box was a red and gold ornament with a sketch in black picturing Matt Damon as the Talented Mr. Ripley. Who else but Dash would delight in a Christmas decoration displaying the face of a celebrated literary serial killer and give it to his girlfriend as a present? The present only made me adore Dash more. (The literary hero part, not the serial killer part.)

In February, I had placed the gift box in the Christmas decorations storage box with a sigh of great hope – that Dash and I would still be together when it was time to put the ornament on the tree. And we were. But our relationship was *ephemeral* (finally an SAT word that applied to my life).

It didn't feel real anymore. It felt more like an obligation that somehow had survived till now so we should at least see it through the holidays, because that's where it started. Then we could stop pretending that what had initially felt so right and true now felt . . . still true, but definitely not right.

"Be good to Oscar," said Boomer. He gave the tree a military salute.

"Who's Oscar?" I asked.

"The tree!" Boomer said, like it was obvious and I had maybe offended Oscar by not knowing his name. "Come on, Dash, we don't want to miss previews."

"Where are you fellas going? How far's the walk?" Grandpa asked them with a touch of desperation in his voice. Grandpa's been mostly housebound since the heart attack and the fall. He doesn't have much stamina for walking more than a block or two anymore, so he practically interrogates visitors about their outside activities. Grandpa's not a guy used to having his wings clipped.

Really what Grandpa should have been asking Boomer and Dash was, *How can you be so rude as to deliver this beautiful tree and then just leave before the tree – I mean, Oscar – is properly decorated? What kind of uncouth urchins are you kids nowadays?*

"We're seeing a movie that starts in twenty minutes," said Dash. His face didn't look remotely guilty, despite the fact that he hadn't invited me.

"What movie?" I asked. If Dash was going to see the one movie I was dying to see without me, then that would

24

be the last sign I needed that he and I really were not connecting anymore and maybe we needed an official break. I'd been counting the days till holiday vacation so I could see *Corgi & Bess,* and I'd probably see it at least five times in the theater if I could find the time. Helen Mirren as a centenarian Queen Elizabeth with a supposedly fantastic animatronic corgi at the side of her walker at all times until an unfortunate fireworks display causes the corgi to run off, and frail old Bess and her walker have to find the corgi somewhere on the grounds of the enchanted Balmoral Castle, with countless adventures along the way for both queen and pup? Yes, please! Count me in, repeated viewings, IMAX *and* 3D! I'd seen the trailer enough times to already know it was my favorite movie of the year, but I'd been holding out hope that Dash would give me a date night first-time viewing of it as my Christmas present. Not just the movie – but the time with him.

"We're seeing *The Naughty and the Mice*!" Boomer told Grandpa in the way Boomer had of delivering even the most basic information with an exclamation mark.

To me, Dash said, "I didn't think you'd want to come, so I didn't ask if you wanted a ticket." Dash was right. I didn't want to see the movie because I'd already seen it. I thought *The Naughty and the Mice* was derivative, but Edgar Thibaud loved the Pixar movie about speed demon attic mice who drag-race Matchbox cars when the house's family is asleep.

I didn't tell Dash I'd already seen *The Naughty and the*

Mice, because I had gone to the movie with Edgar Thibaud. It wasn't like me hanging out with Edgar was a big secret – Dash knew that Edgar also volunteered (court-ordered) at Grandpa's rehabilitation center – but I'd neglected to mention that occasionally he and I hung out after hours. Usually just for a coffee, but this was the first time he and I had gone anywhere beyond a café. I didn't know why I went. I didn't even like Edgar Thibaud that much. Well, I liked him fine enough for a scoundrel who was responsible for the death of my pet gerbil in kindergarten. I just didn't trust him. Maybe Edgar was my stealth side-rehabilitation project, Grandpa being my primary and only truly important one. I wanted to help mold Edgar into a good guy, despite the odds, and if seeing a movie with a girl with the full knowledge that she had nothing beyond a platonic interest in him might evolve Edgar, I could make the effort. I told myself that I'd been so busy the last several months, I needed the relief of a dark time-out in a movie theater, even if it was a movie I didn't care about with a person I barely cared about. If I'd seen the movie with Dash, I would have been preoccupied the whole time, wondering, *Is he going to kiss me now? If not, why not?* With Edgar, all I wondered was, *Is he going to ask me to pay for his popcorn?*

"Have fun," I said, and I managed to sound chipper, trying to be a good sport. I could never stay cold to Dash for long. But Dash's leaving stung, like he'd given me the most fabulous gift only to prematurely snatch it away.

"Oh, we will!" Boomer promised, so anxious to leave

he was hurriedly walking backward toward the door, which caused him to bump into a side table with enough force that the lamp on the table crashed to the floor. It was a minor crash – only the lightbulb broke – but the noise was enough to wake the beast that had been napping in my room. Boris, my dog, came racing into the living room and immediately pinned Boomer to the floor.

"Heel!" I commanded Boris. As a breed, bullmastiffs are surprisingly good apartment dwellers for their size because they're not very active. But they are essentially guard dogs, if compassionate ones – they pin intruders down instead of trying to hurt them. Boomer probably didn't know that. I'd look as terrified as Boomer, too, if I had a 130-pound dog pinning me to the ground. "Heel!" I repeated.

Boris got off Boomer and came and sat at my feet, satisfied that I was safe. But the commotion had also coaxed the smallest fur member of the family out of his own sleep and, typically lazy, he arrived late into the living room to assess the situation and secure the area. Grandpa lives with us now that he can't live on his own anymore, and his cat, Grunt, came along with him. True to his name, the cat grunted at Boris, who standing upright is the size of an adult woman but is abjectly terrified of Grandpa's twelve-pound cat. Poor Boris went from a heeling posture to standing up and draping his front paws over my shoulders, whimpering, his dear, wrinkled face looking into mine like, *Protect me, Mama!* I gave Boris's wet nose a kiss and said, "Down, boy. You're fine."

Our apartment is really too small for all these people

and animals. It's a bloody zoo at my home. I wouldn't have it any other way. I mean, maybe I'd like for Grandpa, who used to be so robust and such a man-about-town, not to be so confined to our third-floor apartment because he can't do the stairs more than once per day, and some days not at all. But if having a stream of family members and health-care workers come in and out to help him and visit with him averts Grandpa's worst fear – being moved to a nursing home – I'm all for the zoo situation. The alternative scenario is bleak. Grandpa often proclaims that the only way he'll allow himself to be moved out of his home is lying flat, in a box.

Langston came into the living room from the kitchen and asked, "What happened in here?" and that was Dash's cue to finally leave.

Dash told Langston, "Thanks for the tea and cookies you didn't offer."

Langston said, "You're welcome. Leaving so soon? Wonderful!" Langston stepped to the front door in the foyer to open it. Bewildered Boomer stood up to step out while Dash hesitated for a moment. He looked like he was about to kiss me goodbye, then thought better of it, and instead he patted Boris's head. Boris the traitor licked Dash's hand.

I was sore, but that didn't mean I wouldn't melt when this impossibly handsome guy in the pea coat was sweet to my dog. "We'll have a tree lighting tomorrow night," I said to Dash. "Will you come?" Tomorrow was the fourteenth of December! Tree-lighting day! How had I managed to completely ignore this most important date until Dash literally plopped a tree into my living room? Was it that maybe this year the ceremony felt more like a chore than a reason for cheer?

"Wouldn't miss it," said Dash. Grunt couldn't have cared less about Dash's acceptance of my invitation. Grunt took chase of Boris again, causing Boris to run – directly into a tall pile of books propped up against the living room wall.

This caused Grandpa to yell, "Grunt, come back here!" and Boris to start barking, and Langston to admonish Dash, "Go, already!"

Boomer and Dash left.

I knew Dash was relieved to leave.

My house is always busy. Loud. Boisterous. Pet hairy. Lots of people around.

Dash likes quiet, and order, and would prefer to be alone with his books than hang out with his own family. He's allergic to cats. Sometimes I wonder if he is to me, too.

Sunday, December 14th

A year ago my life was so different. My Grandpa was in such good shape that he went back and forth to Florida, where he had a girlfriend in his senior-citizen apartment complex. I had no pets and no boyfriend. I didn't really understand sadness.

Grandpa's girlfriend died from cancer this past spring, and soon after that, his heart gave out. I knew Grandpa's fall was serious, but in the panic of the moment I didn't take it all in, because I was too preoccupied with the interminable wait for the ambulance, then the ride to the hospital, then calling all the family to let them know what had happened. It wasn't until the next day, when he was stabilized, that I understood how bad it really had been. I'd gone to the hospital cafeteria to pick up some lunch, and when I returned, I saw through the window to his room that Mrs. Basil E., Grandpa's sister and my favorite aunt, had arrived. She's a tall lady and normally a larger-than-life presence, wearing impeccably tailored suits with expensive jewelry, and perfect makeup on her face. But in that moment before she saw me, she was sitting at sleeping Grandpa's bedside, holding his hand, heavy tears causing mascara to streak down into her lipstick.

I've never, ever seen Mrs. Basil E. cry. She looked so small. I felt a sharp gnawing in my stomach and a choking of my heart. I am a glass-half-full kind of gal – I try to always look on the bright side of things – but I couldn't deny the sharp crest of sadness invading my body and soul at the sight of her grief and worry. Suddenly Grandpa's mortality was too real, and how it would feel when he did eventually die felt too alive with possibility.

Mrs. Basil E. placed Grandpa's hand against her face and wept harder, and for a second, I feared Grandpa was dead. Then his hand came to life and gave her a gentle slap, and she laughed. I knew then everything would be okay, for now – but never the same.

That was my entry into sadness, stage one.

Stage two came the next day, and it was so much worse.

How can such a simple kindness change everything?

Dash came to visit me at the hospital. I had bought food at the cafeteria, but wasn't really eating it – I was too distracted by the situation and didn't have an appetite for stale cheese sandwiches or kale chips, what the hospital offered in lieu of potato chips in a mean attempt at being health conscious. Dash must have heard the fatigue – and hunger – in my voice over the phone, because he arrived carrying a pizza from my favorite place, John's. (The John's location in the Village, not the one in midtown. Come *on*!) A John's pizza is my ultimate comfort food, and even if the pie had gone cold during its trek from the restaurant to the hospital, my heart could not have been warmer at the sight of it – and of Dash carrying it to me.

Impulsively, I blurted out, "I love you so much." I wrapped my arms around his back and buried my head in his neck, covering it in kisses. He laughed, and said, "If I'd known a pizza would get this response, I'd have brought it a lot earlier."

He didn't say *I love you* back.

I hadn't realized I felt it until I said it. I hadn't been talking just about him bringing me the pizza.

When I told Dash *I love you so much,* I meant: *I love you for your kindness and your snarliness. I love you for grossly over-tipping waitstaff when using your dad's credit card to "pay it forward." I love the way you look when reading a book – content and dreamy, off in another world. I love*

how you suggested I never read a Nicholas Sparks book,
and when I did read one because I was curious, and then
read some more, I love you for how confused and offended
and downright angry you were. Not that I'd read them, but
that I adored them. I love debating literary snobbery with
you, and that you can at least recognize that even if you
don't like "pandering, insincere, faux romantic garbage,"
that lots of other people – including your girlfriend – do. I
love you for loving my great-aunt almost as much as I do.
I love how much brighter and sweeter and more interesting
my life has been since you've been a part of it. I love you
for answering the call of a red notebook once upon a time.

Grandpa lived, but a piece of me felt like it died that day, for having the joy of realizing I truly loved somebody so quickly deflated by experiencing the feeling alone.

Dash still hasn't said it back.

I never said it to Dash again.

I don't hold it against him – really, I don't. He's lovely and attentive to me, and I know he likes me. A lot. Sometimes I wish he wouldn't seem so surprised about that.

I said *I love you so much*, and in that instant I meant it with every fiber of my being, but since the moment passed unreciprocated, I've tried to have a little more distance from Dash. I can't make him feel something he doesn't feel, and I don't want to get hurt trying, so I decided to let my love for him simmer on the back burner of my heart, to allow me to be more casual and undemanding of him up front.

It's helped that I've been so busy. I've spent so little time with Dash lately that it's almost stopped hurting. I haven't been actively trying to fall out of love; it's just happened by default. When I'm not in school, I have schoolwork or SAT-prep classes, soccer practice and soccer games, taking Grandpa to physical therapy and doctor's appointments and to visit with his friends. There's the grocery shopping and cooking that Mom and Dad are too busy to do lately because they have new academic jobs. They're not working in another country anymore, but they might as well be; the closest job Mom could get on such short notice was a part-time English teacher gig at a community college in Way Outsville, Long Island, and Dad commutes to a headmaster job at a boarding school in God Only Knows Where, Connecticut. Langston shares the Grandpa responsibilities, but when it comes to housework, he helps only in the half-assed way dudes do. (Obviously that peeves me if I feel compelled to curse.) There's my dog-walking business. My services have become so in demand that Mrs. Basil E. calls me Lily Mogul instead of Lily Bear now. With everything else going on, trying to find time with Dash can feel more like an obligation than a joy.

I'm overwhelmed.

Childish Lily Bear is a distant memory. I feel like in the last year I went from a very young sixteen to a very old seventeen.

*

I've been so busy, I royally screwed up the hasty present I

made to give Dash at my small tree-lighting party. I'd been working on it since the beginning of the year but set it aside when Grandpa's troubles began. I sighed, looking at its resurrection so many months later. My brother laughed.

"It's not *that* bad, is it, Langston?" I said.

"It's . . ." He hesitated too long. "Sweet." Langston pulled the emerald green sweater over his head and then tugged on its looseness. "But Dash is probably close to the same size as me, and this sweater is way too big. Should we presume you'll be resuming your annual holiday cookie drive to fatten Dash up?"

The sweater had been a Christmas gift to our dad several years ago, from the Big & Tall store. Never worn, still in the box. I was repurposing the sweater, but the snowflake-patterned red fabric insert I'd sewn onto the front was original artwork. On it, I'd needlepointed two turtledoves perched together on a tree branch. The left turtledove's belly had DASH sewn on it, and the right's said LILY.

I couldn't deny the visual once my brother was wearing the sweater. I needed to remove the turtledoves insert and sew it on something else, like a hat or scarf. They don't really deserve a sweater, even if you call them something fake adorable like *turtledoves*. It had been a big disappointment to me to learn that turtledoves are basically pigeons who emit gentle purring sounds. I want to think that's cute because I love all animals, but I am a New Yorker and I know: Pigeons are not cute. They're nuisances.

I'm really not feeling Christmas if I'm taking my

grump out on noisy birds who symbolize the season. I told Langston, "You're right, it looks awful. I can't give it to Dash."

"*Please* give it to Dash," Langston said.

The doorbell rang. I said, "Take off the sweater, Langston. Our guests are arriving."

I checked myself in the foyer mirror and smoothed down my hair, hoping I looked presentable. I was wearing my favorite Christmas outfit, a green felt skirt with reindeer figures sewn on the front, and a red T-shirt with the words DON'T STOP BELIEVIN' circling a picture of Santa Claus. The food was here, the lights had been strung around Oscar's ample branches, the animals were confined to my bedroom as a courtesy to our guests. Christmas could begin. Magic could happen.

I wondered if it would be Dash's father at the door. I really thought that if Dash and his dad spent more time together, they'd like each other more, and a small, unassuming party to launch Christmas could be just the occasion to help them along. I'd sent an invite last night to his mom first, but she declined, saying she had a client meeting at the same time. So this morning I had the thought to invite Dash's dad instead.

It was a surprise, then, to open the door and see Dash standing between his mother and father. "Guess who I ran into?" he said.

I don't think his parents have been in the same room together since Dash was a child and had to testify in court during their divorce.

Dash did not have a party face. Neither did his parents.

Finally, cold had arrived for Christmas.

3
DASH

Henpecked

Sunday, December 14th

I knew that if you put Lily into the most elaborate X-ray machine ever devised, and if you scoured the resulting X-ray with the most powerful microscope available in all the universe, you wouldn't find a single bad intention in any bone in her body. I knew the matter at hand was a mistake born of ignorance, not cruelty or mischief. I knew there was no way for her to understand the cosmic scale of her failure.

But, holy shit, I was pissed.

Bad enough that as I was leaving my mother's apartment, Mom called out, "Where are you going? I'm coming with you!"

Okay, I thought. *Mom and Lily have always gotten along. I've always been happy about that. And it's great that Lily wants to share her tree lighting with a wide range of people. Go with it.*

I even chose not to mind when my mother said, "Are you really going to wear that?" and made me put on a tie.

This was probably the first mother-son outing we'd had since puberty had ousted mother-son outings from my to-do list. Still, I tried to rise to the occasion. We chitchatted on the subway about what her reading group had chosen that month. After I professed a complete ignorance about the works of Ann Patchett, we found our way to other subject matter, like the fact that I was going to stay around for New Year's while she and my stepfather were heading out of town. It was fine.

But then we got to Lily's subway stop, and at the top of the stairs, Mom gripped my arm and said, "No. That can't be – no."

At first I thought, *What a coincidence. Of all the places Dad chose to be this afternoon, he happens to be here, in our way.*

Then I saw he was holding a present . . . and it dawned on me that the afternoon was exquisitely fucked.

This registered with my mother, too.

"Lily couldn't possibly have . . . ?" she asked.

The problem was, I didn't have to answer. We both knew it was possible.

"Oh no," Mom said. Then, punctuating each word with a deep breath, "No. No. *No.*"

I know plenty of children of divorce who are sad about the turn of events that turned their family into rubble. But I have never been one of them. Even a casual observer could see that my parents brought out the worst in each other – and I was hardly a casual observer. When things fell apart – I was nine – it felt like a full-time job to observe the way my parents acted around each other. They both thought they were arming themselves with their strengths, but really they were just grabbing for amplified versions of their weaknesses. A seesaw of panic and rage from my mother. A swirl of arrogance and righteous indignation from my father. I tried not to take sides, but ultimately my father's meanness was far worse than my mother's need. He'd done little to disrupt the pattern since.

Lily knew how I felt. She knew I kept a wide demilitarized zone between my parents. It was the only way to prevent constant warfare on my father's end, and hurt on my mother's.

Now she was hurt. Just seeing him, she was hurt.

"I had no idea," I told her.

"I know," she said. Then, after a clear moment of decision, she started walking forward, following my father.

"You don't have to do this," I told her. "Really. I'll explain to Lily. She'll understand."

Mom smiled at me. "We can't let the terrorists win, Dash. I'm going to this tree lighting whether your father is there or not."

She even picked up her pace, so by the time we got to Lily's block, we were only a few feet behind my father. Characteristically, he wasn't looking back.

"Dad," I said, finally, as we got to the front steps.

He turned and saw me first. Put on his Father Face. (It never quite fit.) Then he looked next to me and flashed some genuine surprise.

"Oh," he said.

"Yeah," my mom replied. "*Oh*."

We stood there clucking for a minute, pleasantries without any feeling of pleasantness. Mom asked after Dad's new-but-not-that-new wife. Dad asked after Mom's new-but-not-that-new husband. It felt surreal – the names didn't match the voices that usually said them. I was at a loss – and the loss was one I had grown up with. It was not something I wanted to get any closer to.

The present that Dad was holding was wrapped – maybe by the wife, maybe by the shop. Whatever the case, it showed more care than I'd received in years. I got checks – when I got anything at all. She always signed the birthday cards for him.

Even before Lily answered the door, Mom and Dad started to peck at each other – Dad saying, "I didn't know you were going to be here," and Mom saying, "Why wouldn't I be here?" – until I pecked at both of them to be quiet. I knew Lily's whole family would be here, and the last thing I wanted was for them to see how rocky the surface of my gene pool was.

Lily opened the door and I had to remind myself: *She had no idea she had no idea she had no idea*. So I didn't scream. I just said, "Guess who I ran into?"

A different girlfriend would have answered my sarcastic salvo with one of her own. *Krampus?* Lily might have said. Or Scrooge. Or Judah Frickin' Maccabee. But that wasn't what Lily was going to answer. Instead she asked, "Can I take your coats?" Only, none of us were wearing coats.

Instead of answering, my father held out his present. "For you, my dear," he said to Lily.

"I would have brought something," my mother quickly interjected, "but Dash told me it wasn't that kind of party."

My father laughed. "Typical!" he said to Lily, as if she knew as well as he how bad I was at figuring out what kind of party a party was.

"It really *isn't* that kind of a party," Lily said. "But thank you anyway."

And my father, true to form, said, "Well, if it's not that kind of party, I can always take the present back." He lunged to take it from her, and then pulled away, laughing again. "God, it was just a joke, people," he said once he realized he was the only one laughing.

"I'll put this in my room," Lily said. I understood from the way she said it that I was meant to follow. But there was no way I could leave my mom alone.

"We'll go in and meet everyone," I said.

"Oh. Okay. I'll be right in."

In most situations involving stress and strife, the last person you'd want to add into the mix is an ex. But in this case, when I walked into the living room and saw Sofia, all I felt was gratitude. She and my mother had always gotten along well.

"Come say hi to Sofia," I said, leading my mother over. "I told you she came back from Barcelona, right? Why don't you ask her if that cathedral is finished yet?"

41

"So good to see you!" Sofia's smile was wide, and her eyes were reading my SOS. "I don't really know anyone else here – Boomer's late, and Lily's been running around getting everything together. It's great to see a familiar face."

My mother smiled back. "You have no idea."

"I'll be right back," I said. Because there was still the bomb-disposal task of managing my father.

He was starting to talk to Langston, and I didn't have to hear what he was saying to know that every word out of his mouth was confirming Langston's worst view of my lineage.

". . . no reason to look so smug. I have every reason to be here. I was invited, for Christ's sake."

"I'm sure Lily invited you, sir," Langston replied. "But I don't think she did it for Christ."

This flustered my father for a moment, and Langston used this pause to say "I have to go see a man about a reindeer" and bolt to another room. My father immediately started scouring the room for his next conversational hostage.

"Dad," I said. "Over here."

I knew that if there was anyone in this room who could handle my jackass father, it was Mrs. Basil E. I wouldn't need to say a word of explanation to her – from her perch on Lily's sofa, she would have already taken in the situation with a knowledge approaching omniscience. I knew she didn't suffer fools gladly, but she'd gladly make a fool suffer.

"There's someone I want you to meet," I told my dad. "This is Lily's aunt."

My father eyed her, and paid her little more mind than he would an old lady trying to cross the street. He was prepared to walk right past.

"So," Mrs. Basil E. said, eyeing him with both curiosity and a desire to kill a cat, "you're this rapscallion's father?"

My father straightened up a little at that. "Guilty as charged. Or at least that's the story his mother told me."

"Oh – and you're rakish as well! I've often found it helpful to have a shovel around when you're dealing with a rake."

"I'm not sure I follow . . ."

"And I, sir, am not very sure you lead. But no matter. Why don't you sit down next to me? As little as I expect I'll enjoy your company, it will gratify me greatly to see you out of the way. Lily takes these celebrations very seriously, and in my estimation, you are currently the person in the room with the highest likelihood of ruining this one. Let's make sure that doesn't happen."

Mrs. Basil E. didn't exactly pat the seat next to her. Instead she seemed to cast a spell on the cushion so it wouldn't be tainted when my father sat down.

"I didn't have to be here, you know," he mumbled. I almost felt sorry for him. But not quite.

"That reflects well on you," Mrs. Basil E. conceded. "Now don't alter that reflection with further speech. Let's sit and watch the others."

Powerless, my father obliged.

"Get your father some cider," Mrs. Basil E. ordered.

"Make it a double," Dad said.

"The cider is entirely devoid of alcohol," Mrs. Basil E. disclaimed.

"But still – it's cider," my father replied, finally earning a slight glimmer of her respect.

I performed this errand with haste – handing my father two mugs, neither of which read WORLD'S GREATEST FATHER. Then I went in search of Lily, who had yet to return.

First I checked the kitchen, but only found her father there, looking as if he was trying to remember which appliance was the stove. Then I ventured down the hall to see if the bathroom door was closed; it wasn't.

It was quiet as I got near her room – so quiet, I assumed she wouldn't be there. But when I peeked in, there she was, all alone. She wasn't looking for anything. Wasn't checking her phone. Wasn't making a last-minute change to her holiday playlist. Instead she was sitting on the edge of her bed, staring out at the edge of the world. Lost in thought, or thinking thoughts that would be lost the minute I said her name and she snapped to attention, fugue-state fugitive. It was disturbing to see her like this, but I still wasn't sure I should disturb her. There's an alone that calls out for rescue – but this appeared to be an alone that wanted to be left alone.

I was going to quietly head back to the party, but at the moment of my first retreat, she slipped out of wherever it was she had been and turned to see me in the doorway. Maybe she'd known I was there all along. Maybe I had no idea what she was thinking.

"Dash," she said, as if we both needed to be reminded who I was.

"The party?" I replied. "Is there anything I can do?"

Lily shook her head. "I think everything's ready. It's not really a party. It's just a tree lighting."

I saw my father's present unopened on her desk. I picked it up and shook it. Something rolled around inside.

"Well, at least it's not a check," I said. "It required at least some thought. His or someone else's." I shook it more furiously. "I hope it's not breakable."

"Stop," Lily said.

I stopped.

"I have something for you," she said. "You don't have to open it now. And you don't have to wear it if you don't want to. Ever. I just – well, it's just something I thought I'd give to you. But you're under no obligation."

"It's a leather miniskirt, isn't it?" I asked. "You killed me a cow and turned it into a miniskirt for me!"

From the horror on her face, you would have thought I'd guessed correctly. Which, I'm sure, led to some horror on my face. Which lightened Lily up a little.

"No cows were hurt in the making of this sweater," she assured me.

And I thought, *Oh boy. Sweater.*

It's not that I didn't think Lily could knit a sweater. I thought Lily could make anything she set her mind on making, whether it be a five-tier cake or a macramé Madonna. But sweaters . . . living in New York City, I had a very complicated relationship to sweaters. When you were outside, they were fine, even preferable, keeping away the big chill. But inside? When the temperature suddenly skyrocketed to ninety degrees? *Sweagatory* – sweaty purgatory.

Lily went to the base of her bookshelf and picked up a tissue-paper-wrapped package. "Here," she said, handing it over.

I stopped to ponder what kind of wild night between a Kleenex and a piece of 8-by-11 had led to the birth of tissue paper. Then I ripped it to shreds and opened up the sweater within.

The first thing I noticed was how huge it was – at least two X's past XL, with room for an extra reindeer if it happened to need shelter underneath. Then I noticed how *Christmas* it was – even though Lily was giving me a sweater for Christmas, it hadn't occurred to me that it might be a *Christmas sweater.* The snowflake on the front looked like it had been woven by a spider who'd gotten a little too fly-drunk the night before. And then there were the birds. Doves, I thought. With our names on them. Lily's dove had a sprig of olive tree in its mouth. Mine was just kind of lurking.

"Oh, Lily," I said. "I mean, *wow.*"

I knew she must have spent a lot of time on it, so I said, "You must have spent so much time on it!"

I knew it matched her own Santa-positive outfit. So I said, "We match!"

I knew it had been a hard year for her, so I mustered full-blast cheer to say, "I'm going to put it on right now!"

She started to tell me I didn't need to do that, but I blocked out all her protestations with the miles of sacrificial yarn that passed over my ears. When I finally found the head hole, I surfaced and took a breath. From far away, I must have looked like a deranged mitten.

"I love it!" I said, rolling up the sleeves so that my knuckles could get some air.

"You do not love it," Lily said. "I told you not to wear it. It was the thought that was supposed to count."

"No," I said. "This is much more than the thought. I have never, ever had anyone knit me a sweater before. Not my parents. Not my grandparents. Not the great-aunts in Florida who have way, way too much time on their hands. Certainly none of my friends. This is special to me."

"I didn't knit it all. I just . . . repurposed."

"Even better! Less of a wool footprint left on the environment! That's brilliant!"

I was in danger of putting the *clamato* in *exclamation* – not even remotely palatable – so I dialed it down.

"Really," I told her, reaching over for her hand, making her look at me to see my sincerity. "This is one of the best things I've ever gotten. I'll wear it with pride. Dash-and-Lily pride."

Once upon a time, this would have made her smile. Once upon a time, this would have made her happy.

I wanted us to be upon that time.

"You really don't have to wear it," she said once again.

"I know."

Before she could say it another time, before the sweat line moved below my forehead, where I could feel it gathering, I walked to the door. Turning back, I asked, "You coming?" Then I added, "I'm sure my mom would love to talk to you. And your father's looking a little lost in the kitchen."

Now Lily's attention seemed to focus. "My father? In the kitchen? That's not – I mean, he only goes in there when he needs a snack." She stood up, stepped forward. "If he's trying to help, we need to stop him. And was my mother in there? She's even worse."

"I didn't see your mom," I assured her.

We walked down the hallway. When we got to the kitchen, we found it empty.

"I don't think he did any damage," Lily concluded after a quick scan. Then she looked at me. "And speaking of damage – I'm sorry about your parents. I was caught up in the spirit of inviting people, I guess. I honestly don't know what I was thinking. I got confused between what I wanted to happen and what I should have known would happen. I've been doing that a lot lately. I know it's not helpful."

"It's fine," I promised her – but that didn't land well, because we both knew it wasn't particularly true. So I rephrased. "I'm sure it will be fine now that the initial shock has worn off. They'll stay on separate sides of the room. Mrs. Basil E. will keep my dad in check. If anyone can do it, she can."

This appeared to be the case when we returned to the living room. Boomer had arrived and was talking animatedly with Sofia and my mom. His hand was on her back (Sofia's, not my mom's) in that I-must-show-everyone-we're-linked-by-taking-it-beyond-metaphor way that people in new couples have. If I'd done that to Sofia when we were courting, she probably would have swatted it away, called it condescending. But with Boomer, she seemed to like it. Or at least to not think about it. Somehow his touch had become natural to her.

My mom noticed this. I saw her see it. I had no doubt she would have liked my stepfather to be here to back her up in the same way, instead of on some business trip.

Meanwhile, Mrs. Basil E. was *tsk*ing my father into submission. I hated that he seemed to be enjoying her company nonetheless.

I was aware of the way the room shifted to accommodate my sweater. There were looks, for sure. But as soon as the laughter came into a person's eyes, another knowledge would counterbalance – the big contextual clue that I was standing next to Lily, and therefore this sweater must be something Lily had done. Because of that – and solely because of that – the laughter died before Lily could hear it. Nobody in the room wanted her to feel anything but right, anything but loved. Although, in fairness, I could tell from his eyes that Grandpa found the whole thing hysterical.

I don't think Lily noticed any of this. She was considering the tree instead, adjusting a candle holder she'd hung from a middle branch. "I guess it's time," she said, more to herself than to me. She sought out Langston in the crowd, and the two of them exchanged a wordless go-ahead. Langston's boyfriend Benny gave him a little squeeze, and Langston stepped forward.

"Can I have everyone's attention?" he yelled. All the animals in the manger fell quiet. There had to be at least twenty people in the room now – cousins and distant cousins and family friends who'd attained cousin status – a kind of middle-class knighthood. It was only the people I'd brought into Lily's life – my parents, Boomer, Sofia – who were new to this ritual. The rest of them were family. We were guests.

Langston continued. "As you all know, we've had a bit of a rough year."

"Speak for yourself!" Grandpa roared.

Langston smiled. "But we're all here, which is the most important thing we can hope for every year. So, without further ado, I hand it off to Lily."

I expected Lily to feel the warmth in the room, the power of having her family gathered together. But instead she still seemed a little lost. "You didn't have to say all that, Langston," she began. "I mean, about the year. That's not why we're here."

An awkward silence followed. Then Boomer yelled, "We're here to light a tree on FIRE!"

This got some titters. Sofia leaned over to explain the tree-lighting concept to him.

"If everyone could get into a circle around the tree, we can get started," Lily said. "For those of you who haven't been a part of this before, we each get a candle, and one person lights the next person's candle. When it gets to Gramps, he'll light the candle on the tree, and I'll turn on all the electric lights. Oh, and thank you to Dash and Boomer for the tree."

"Go, Oscar!" one of the two of us cheered.

People looked around the room for Oscar. He did not take a bow.

I looked over at my mom, who had summoned up her best fake smile.

I looked over at my dad, who looked mildly embarrassed.

"Come on, people!" Langston shouted. "The lady wants a circle, so let's give her a circle."

People made a very loose ring around the tree. In the shuffle, I ended up between Sofia and my mother. Boomer took his place on my mother's other side. Then, in order to dodge a particularly garrulous cousin, my father stepped next to Boomer. Lily handed out red, green, and white candles. Then she went to turn off the lights and cue up "White Christmas" on the sound system. As Bing did his thing, Lily lit her candle, then touched it to her mother's until the flame held. Then her mother did the same with Lily's father. The circle began. Nobody said a word. We just traced the progress of the light, awaited our turn. Grandpa took about a minute longer than he should have to get out of his chair to take his place, but when it was his turn, his hand was steady as he passed his fire to Langston. Langston went wick-to-wick with Benny, who then pirouetted to face Sofia. Sofia smiled and cupped the flame as she turned to pass it to me.

Boomer, who had never really had a girlfriend before, clearly felt it was his boyfriendly obligation to be the recipient of Sofia's flame. He jumped from his place and stepped in between me and Sofia. Sofia, not wanting to disrupt anything, dutifully touched her candle to his. I watched, then held steady as Boomer did a little dance over to me, cooing at the flame to stay alive long enough to make my acquaintance. Boomer lit my candle, then I turned and faced my stricken mother. Boomer's jump had put her right next to my father. And it was too late for any of us to fix it without making it a big deal.

It's fine, I assured myself. *My parents are adults. They can act like adults.*

My mother's hand was shaking so much, I was worried the candle was going to fall. It took us three tries for her to be steady enough to transfer the flame.

"It's okay," I whispered to her. "You're doing great."

She nodded so slightly that I was sure I was the only one who could recognize it as a nod. Then she turned to her ex-husband and extended her candle.

For a second, I thought it was going to be okay. For a second, their candles were touching and it was just like it had been with everyone else. For a second, my mother was looking at her candle while my father was looking at my mother.

Then my father opened his mouth.

My mother wasn't looking. She didn't see it coming. When my father said, "And here I was, thinking you'd never light my fire again," she wasn't prepared. The shock that hit was real, and it was powerful. She recoiled. And as she did, her candle fell. As she called him a bastard, the flame hit a section of the Sunday paper that someone had left under the tree. As he told the room she had never been able to take a joke, the floor burst into flame.

I thought everyone would react, and maybe they would have, but I was the closest person who wasn't an arguing member of my former family, and I was the one who got there first. *Smother the flame*, I thought. *Smother it*. So I belly-flopped onto the paper and the candle that had started this mess. I suffocated the flames. It was only as I was mid-flop that it occurred to me that this was a stupid reaction. I half expected to set myself on fire. But the smothering worked. I robbed the situation of its oxygen. I put out the fire my father had started.

I was conscious of Lily screaming. Langston yelling. Then Boomer in the air, to smother the smotherer. "Close your eyes!" someone yelled. I did, and was doused with a foamy, chemical substance just as Boomer landed on top of me.

Everyone was quiet for a moment. Then:

"You can open your eyes."

I did, and found Mrs. Basil E. standing over me and

Boomer, with a sizable fire extinguisher. We were covered in foam.

My mother kneeled down beside me. "Are you okay?"

I nodded, my chin squishing into the carpet.

"Boomer," my mother said gently, "I think you might be crushing him."

Accurate!

Benny and Langston helped Boomer up. Then Langston reached down for me. When I got to my feet, he said, "Oh, that's not good."

Was I hurt? Was there a burn so severe I couldn't feel it?

No. I was fine.

But I'd murdered the sweater.

I looked down and saw a smear of wax and a field of singe. My dove looked like a toasted marshmallow. Lily's looked like it had flown way too close to the sun. And the snowflake had undergone a precipitous meltdown.

I looked up and saw Lily. Everything I needed to know was right there in her eyes. She wanted to cry, but wouldn't let herself. Which was worse than her actually crying.

"I'm so sorry," I told her.

"No," she said. "It really doesn't matter."

Suddenly everyone was talking. The lights were back on. My mother was taking deep breaths. And my father . . .

My father was gone.

Mrs. Basil E. insisted on inspecting me for any "errant burns." Benny started to refill people's cider. People blew out the candles they were holding and put them down on the floor where the newspaper had been. Lily flicked on the tree's electric lights. Nobody oohed or aahed.

I had no idea how to make it better.

We all rallied – tried to fill that apartment with a joyful noise. But mostly it felt like we were trying to cover up another noise, an uncertainty that had crept into our party and wouldn't leave no matter how unwanted we made it feel.

I'd been planning to stay later – to help Lily clean up, to talk about everything that had happened, to try to turn it into a comedy so it wouldn't linger as a tragedy. But as the cousins started to exit for their respective boroughs and Sofia and Boomer left for an evening date, Lily summarily dismissed me, telling me that I should probably head home with my mom. I knew she was right, but at the same time, I worried that Lily might need my attention more than my mom.

This was especially true after Mom and I left, and it became quickly clear that my mother Didn't Want To Talk About It. When we emerged from our subway station back home, my phone buzzed with a text from my father.

Sorry 2 have left. Seemed best.

I refused to reply.

Which seemed best.

Monday, December 15th
I texted Lily later that night after the party, to check in.

No response.

The next day, I texted her a few times during the school day. At first to check in. Then to make sure she hadn't checked out.

It wasn't like her to fail to respond.

I asked her if she wanted to get together after school. I called her and left a message along the same lines.

Nothing.

By the end of the night, all the birds had gone quiet.

4
LILY

Rogue Coddled Bird

Tuesday, December 16th

Christmas was still over a week away, but it was already ruined. I hate to use such harsh language, but everything felt motherfudging suck.

I woke up to the sound of my parents fighting, loudly. Boris lay at the foot of my bed, his paws covering his eyes, whimpering from the angry tones coming from the next room.

Mom: "I will not move to Connecticut!"

Dad: "Do you *want* me to be unemployed? I left an excellent job in Fiji because of your dad."

Mom: "You hated that job! You hated Fiji!"

Dad: "*You* hated Fiji. I wouldn't have left the job so soon if *you* hadn't insisted."

Mom: "My father had a heart attack! We couldn't be so far away!"

Dad: "Your father has four siblings, your brother, and a trove of grandchildren and nieces and nephews who could have cared for him just fine. Even if your brother says he'll help but can never bother to budge from his vacation cabin in Maine when we need him."

Mom: "You hate my family!"

Dad: "I don't hate your family. How dare you accuse me of that? I just don't know why in our twenty-six years of marriage we've never been allowed to live farther than a five-mile radius from them. Except for a few god–" – I covered my ears for the rest of the word that rhymed with *slam* – "months in Fiji."

Mom (now shrieking): "I WILL NOT MOVE TO CONNECTICUT!"

(The f-word that isn't *fudge* also appeared in that shriek, but my ears redacted it.)

Just then my phone *ding*ed with a text message from Dash. *I'm so sorry about the sweater! Are you okay?*

I certainly was not okay. Connecticut?!?! How was that distant place a conceivable option? I knew headmasters usually lived on the grounds at boarding schools, but the school that hired Dad had said it was fine if he lived in the city and commuted, even if it was a two-hour commute each way. He could work on the train. (Or so Grandpa and I had been told soon after my parents returned from Fiji. Perhaps it hadn't been a whole truth, but a convenient fib to get us through the early days of Grandpa's recovery.)

I'd heard my parents fight before, obviously. But their "fights" were more like typical old-people bickering, and they usually shushed it if Langston or I was in hearing range. But this fight? It was loud, it was epic, and it was scary.

The fight would never have happened if it hadn't been for the other night. Dash's parents must have infected mine with their dysfunction and callous disregard for each other. One could also say it was my fault for having invited both of Dash's parents, but that was actually their fault. I invited his mom, who declined, so I thought it was safe to invite his dad instead, as a gesture of goodwill that this stupid season is supposed to be all about. It was Dash's mom's fault for saying she couldn't come and then coming anyway, and Dash's fault for bringing her, and Dash's dad's fault for even agreeing to come just to make a point that he could be all supportive dad-like for once in his relationship with Dash. It was Dash's fault for running into his dad on the street while he was with his mom, but still continuing on to the tree-lighting party. Dash had to have known no good would come of it. Those people together are toxic. No wonder Dash is so snarly.

But now it was me who felt snarly. "BE QUIET!" I shouted. I hurled my phone against the wall I shared with Mom and Dad. Stupid text messages about sweaters. Stupid fights.

That stupid sweater, charred and ruined. Not even the stupid cat would sleep on it. That sweater was such a symbol of everything wrong between me and Dash. Trying too hard plus good intentions does not necessarily equal happy fairy-tale endings.

Fairy tales aren't even real. They're stupid, like everything else. Fudge. STRESS!

After the thud of my phone against the wall, my parents' voices lowered, but their arguing continued. I could hear it in occasional loud intonations of "*Your* fault!" and "Just how many people exist in this marriage anyway?"

I didn't want to get out of bed, but I didn't want to stay at home and listen to this upsetting nonsense any longer. Connecticut?!? What could that place have to recommend it besides New Haven pizza?

My bedroom door opened. "Can I come in?" Langston whispered.

"Can you *knock* first?" I said, irritated. My brother loses his mind if I don't knock before going into his room in case his boyfriend is there and they want to be private, but he never knocks first at my bedroom door, since it's always safe to assume nothing too private is happening in there. That's its own kind of annoying assumption, because the assumption is right. My family can barely tolerate me having a boyfriend, and that's only because he's broody but bookishly non-threatening, and we don't see each other that much, and he's never allowed in my room with the door closed, and I still have a curfew.

Langston almost smiled. "Ha ha," he said. He closed my bedroom door behind him and hopped on my bed. He was still wearing his pj's even though I knew he was supposed to be at an early morning class about now. It was almost like Christmas mornings when we were kids, both of us huddled on my bed wearing our pj's, waiting for our parents to come in and lead us outside to the presents. From my bed, Langston and I would eavesdrop on our parents' Christmas-morning squabbling in the next room. But those "fights" were more lighthearted jabs, like one of them said they'd finished wrapping the presents but hadn't, or one of them said they bought coffee the day before but hadn't. Oh, the good ole days. Before "Connecticut" was a mean, hateful word that augured bad things to come. When life was so innocent.

God, I love presents. Especially when they come with fresh-baked Christmas scones, drizzled in red and white frosting. I don't even mind if there's no coffee. Sometimes it's impossible not to remember how much I love Christmas, and then my heart pangs extra hard for how everything is fudging suck this year. I just can't get into the holiday mood no matter how hard everyone else tries to coax me there.

It might be all the coaxing that's holding me back from getting there. These feelings have to happen organically. Forced gaiety is the worst. I need sincerity to feel the season.

"What's going on?" I said to Langston.

"I think it's pretty apparent what's going on!" he said, but not jokily. He looked too serious.

"Are they getting divorced?" I asked. I assumed that's what happened to parents who fought so loudly. I wondered if I should suggest to Dash that he get his hearing tested to check for any ear damage caused by exposure to his crazy parents' fights when he was a kid. Probably not. Knowing

Dash, when they fought, he probably wore headphones while he was lost in a book, even as a little man.

"Hardly," said Langston. "It's just a rough patch."

"Like you and Benny have?" My brother and his boyfriend break up about every other month, and then there's a flurry of five thousand text messages, and crying and heart emojis, and Robyn songs, and then they can't live without each other again.

"There's something I have to tell you," Langston announced.

"They *are* getting divorced!" I cried out.

"Shut up, not so loud. Of course they're not. They're fighting because I told them last night what I'm about to tell you, and I think it tripped their alarm on other issues."

I gasped. "You have cancer? And you can only be treated in Connecticut!" Cruel universe, why, why, why? My brother hasn't even finished college yet. Don't take him away so soon.

"Would you just shut up and let me finish? No, I don't have cancer, and if I did, why would I go to Connecticut for treatment when I live in the city?"

"Exactly!"

"Listen, Lily . . . I wanted you to hear it first from me and not Mom and Dad. I'm moving out. Benny and I got an apartment together."

I laughed. "Now's not the time for jokes, Langston."

"I'm not joking," said my brother. A traitor, just like Dash. Pretending like everything's okay and status quo when clearly it's not.

I realize there are much worse things happening in the world, but my East Village apartment is the only place I've ever lived. It and the people in it *are* my world, and it felt like my world was ending. My brother was moving out. They hadn't told me yet, but Mrs. Basil E. had offered to have Grandpa come live with her. That left my parents open to possibly leaving the city – if they could just figure out what to do about me in such a way that didn't cause me to have a meltdown. (Funny how everyone worried over that dilemma *without asking me*. Funny, and infuriating.)

The world as I knew and loved it was disintegrating, and maybe Dash and I were, too. I could see how hard Dash was trying, and it only made me feel more distant from him. He shouldn't have to try so hard. It should just be or not be. As if he also knew it, Boris had just finished ripping Dash's charred gift sweater to bits, and I didn't even care. I was almost glad. It seemed the appropriate way to dispose of the sweater once and for all.

My parents were late for work after their argument, and they didn't stop to say goodbye to me, or sorry for ruining my day. Langston left to go thrift store shopping for new furniture for his new apartment rather than console me through the pain of his announcement that he was deserting me for his boyfriend. Grandpa was still asleep, and probably wouldn't wake up till his home health worker came to check on him later in the morning.

Grudgingly, I put on my uniform and prepared to leave

for school, even though I was late and Mom hadn't left me a note to excuse the tardy. I gave Boris a kiss and told him to nap for the day until I got home, and I reminded him not to pin down Grandpa's visiting nurse again, because she carries mace in her purse and doesn't like sudden movements. I was about to leave my apartment when Edgar Thibaud's number appeared on my phone, calling me on FaceTime.

"What?" I answered. I sat on my bed. Edgar's face appeared on my phone screen, looking sweaty and disheveled. He'd become quite the club kid in the last year, and he was probably calling me as his previous night's shenanigans were ending and my already ruined day was just beginning.

"Lily! Dude! Ramen emergency."

"Excuse me?" I could see a group of club kids laughing and stumbling around on the street behind him.

"We need ramen to soak up the drunk in our tummies. But every ramen place we went in Koreatown after karaoke wasn't open this early."

He did not deserve my help, but I didn't feel like going to school just yet, so I didn't hang up on him. "Where are you now?"

"How do you expect me to know that?"

"Put your camera on the nearest street sign instead of your face." That face. So stubbly and amber wolf-eyed and full-mouthed. Also, stupid.

His camera wobbled first to his feet, wearing men's black and white saddle shoes and showing a glimpse of pink-and-black plaid pants ("Urban *Caddyshack*" is how Edgar Thibaud describes his personal style). Then the camera dropped to the ground, was lifted up again to reveal a fire hydrant that looked freshly peed on, and then up and over to a street sign. Bowery and Canal.

I did my mental food-map brain scan and said, "Great N.Y. Noodletown, Bowery and Pell. They open early." I only knew this drunk info because it was my brother and Benny's favorite post-dancing-the-night-away spot – when they weren't broken up.

"I'll never find it," Edgar Thibaud whined. "Come help me."

"I'll send you a link. I have to get to school." I sighed. "Even though I don't wanna go."

"So don't," Edgar said, and hung up on me.

For once, Edgar was right. I was always such a good girl. I got good grades and I tried to take care of everyone and I never missed class or soccer practice or dog-walking appointments or SAT-prep class or volunteer work. I ate a lot of carbs like pizza and bagels, but threw vegetables on them when I remembered, and if enough cheese was involved. I didn't smoke, drink, do drugs, or do anything too naughty with Dash. I never even said the f-word.

"FUCK!" I yelled. Wow, that felt good. So I said it again. "Fuck, fuck, fuck!" Boris placed his paws over his ears again and refused to look at me.

I sent a quick message to that afternoon's dog-walking clients that I was sick and couldn't tend to their dogs today, along with the contact info for my dog-walking subs. Then I threw my phone on my bed so no one could text or email or call or FaceTime or tag me so I could be whoever I wanted to be today, without distraction or electronic intervention. I hastily left the apartment before I lost my courage to wander the city phoneless, like in olden days.

I had no plan for where I'd go, so I just walked. Roaming the streets of Manhattan on foot has always been one of my favorite ways to find inspiration. There's so much to see and smell (not all of it pleasant, except this time of year, which smells of roasted cashews, crisp air, and gingerbread lattes). It was impossible not to feel exhilarated on a day like today, so sunny and warm, which was annoying for December, but also helpful since I was outside walking and the stores were decorated for the holidays and there was a palpable sense of cheer among my fellow pedestrians.

Truth: There wasn't actually a palpable sense of cheer, but I decided to pretend there was, in hopes the holiday cheer would seep into my troubled soul.

"Don't be such a coddled bird," Langston had said to me this morning after I burst into tears when he said he was moving and I said I wasn't ready for him to go, especially if that meant my parents thought their eldest leaving the nest opened the door for them to kidnap their youngest to Connecticut. Hah! *Coddled bird.* It was the name Langston sometimes teased me with, because of the framed picture on our living room mantelpiece, picturing Grandpa holding five-year-old me in front of that year's Christmas tree, with his sister, Mrs. Basil E., on one side of us, and his twin brothers, Great-Uncle Sal and Great-Uncle Carmine, standing on his other side. In the photo, the siblings are holding beers, their mouths open but not about to drink, because they were serenading their little girl with a Christmas carol. Whenever Langston gets annoyed with our relatives for babying me too much (because I am the youngest of all the grandchildren and, I'm told, the most delightful), he'll look at that picture of the four siblings serenading their baby girl and, to the tune of "The Twelve Days of Christmas," will sing out, *"Four coddle birds"* instead of "four calling birds." Who even knows what the fudge – I mean, fuck! – calling birds are.

I know I am an overprotected, coddled bird, but I'd like to evolve past that. I mean, not to the extent that I don't get generous birthday cash, but a certain amount of independence would be healthy.

I'd walked so far west from the East Village that I'd reached Seventh Avenue and Fourteenth. The universe had obviously landed me at the 1 train station for a reason. I knew exactly where I wanted to go. I hopped the 1 downtown and took it to the end of the line at South Ferry, where I got onto the Staten Island Ferry.

Grandpa isn't one of just four coddle bird siblings. They also have one rogue tribesman: Great-Uncle Rocco, their other brother, who no one talks to except when they have to, because he's not very nice, and he lives in that outer, outer borough known as Staten Island. He might as well live in Connecticut for how far away Staten Island felt. Nobody likes Great-Uncle Rocco, and the feeling is mutual. I always made it my mission to like him, because somebody has to like the people no one else likes or the world would just be hopeless. And the best way to extract holiday cheer, I've found, is to spend some time with the most curmudgeonly person you know, and their grump can't help but force you into feeling good, because it gives you perspective and balance. Maybe that's why I love – I mean, very much like – Dash so much.

Maybe I should have corralled Dash for Lily's Day Off, but everything we did together lately seemed to lead to disaster. A lone, rogue trip to Staten Island was probably a safer bet.

My mom calls the Staten Island Ferry "the poor-woman's cruise," and I could see why. For just the cost of a MetroCard swipe, travel grandeur was achieved. As the boat pushed forward, I marveled at the convergence of rivers and city skyline, and felt my mood immediately brighten. I waved hello to the Statue of Liberty and, as always, worried about Lady Liberty. Her arm must get so tired. I wish she could switch arms sometimes to give the one holding up the torch some relief. Her torch arm is probably way buff, though. Don't mess with her, bad guys.

I was surprised how much I reveled in the aloneness of the day. I so rarely spend time with just myself. The coddle birds who coddled me were probably right. I *was* delightful, at least on a day like today, with no phone to trap me, no responsibilities, alone with my thoughts and the wonder of the water. It was almost Christmas! I could feel the organic inklings of excitement as I remembered one of the poems Mom used to read to us at this time of year, by Henry Wadsworth Longfellow.

The holiest of all holidays are those
Kept by ourselves in silence and apart;
The secret anniversaries of the heart,
When the full river of feeling overflows; –
The happy days unclouded to their close;
The sudden joys that out of darkness start
As flames from ashes; swift desires that dart
Like swallows singing down each wind that blows!
White as the gleam of a receding sail,
White as a cloud that floats and fades in air,
White as the whitest lily on a stream,
These tender memories are; – a fairy tale
Of some enchanted land we know not where,
But lovely as a landscape in a dream.

Once the ferry docked on Staten Island, I took the S62 bus to the island's most important destination, Joe & Pat's, for a most perfect slice of pizza, just as Grandpa taught me. Then I walked over to the gas station on the corner, which is also an auto body shop. Uncle Rocco owns the business. I've caught Grandpa and Mrs. Basil E. reading the Yelp reviews of Uncle Rocco's and laughing. "Crook" is the most common word used in the reviews, but customers also proclaim they won't go anywhere else, because no other shop does as good a job, even if Uncle Rocco price-gouges them.

Uncle Rocco was sitting on a chair outside the auto body shop, wearing a mechanic's uniform and smoking a cigar, despite the regulatory signs on the gas pumps stating that smoking was not allowed on the property. "Hi, Uncle Rocco!" I said. His face scrunched, trying to recognize me.

Even though it was warm, I hadn't been able to resist wearing my favorite red winter hat with the red pom-poms dangling from the ears. I think that's how Uncle Rocco finally placed my face, because I always wear that hat on the one day of the year the family sees him, November 29, when Grandpa and his siblings go to visit their mother's grave in Staten Island, on the anniversary of her death. Thanksgiving followed by that annual cemetery trip are what usually kick off the Christmas season for me, but we hadn't made the journey this year. No one even remembered.

Uncle Rocco frowned. "Did someone die?" he asked me.

"No, but Grandpa had a tough year," I said.

"Hmmph," Uncle Rocco said. "There any other reason you're here?"

"No."

"Then be on your way. I don't give discounts, if you're needing a gas fill-up."

"I don't!" I said, exhilarated. "Merry Christmas!"

Finally. The season had *begun*.

I headed back toward the S62 bus stop to take me back

to the Staten Island Ferry Terminal, but was overwhelmed by the smell of ginger, cinnamon, and sugary goodness at a corner storefront. The store's windows were papered over and there was a FOR LEASE sign on the door. There was no actual bakery business, but the door was open, and I couldn't resist going in. The smell demanded it.

Inside, there were probably a dozen long metal tables, each containing gingerbread houses in various stages of preparation. Half-built churches. Castles needing roofs. Little fairy houses needing retaining walls. On the supply table, there were piles of bags of gumdrops, M&M's, candy canes and peppermint candies, bottles of food coloring, boxes of graham crackers, bowls of icing, and architectural tools my hands ached to use: pliers, paintbrushes, cardboard cutouts. It was heaven. I have no idea what I want to do with my life, but one thing I do know is that I wouldn't mind dedicating it to the pursuit of competitive gingerbread-house making. (The guidance counselor at my high school has informed me this is not a viable option. Dream killer. I'll prove him wrong!)

A young woman wearing a white baker's apron stood over a table of gingerbread cookies, holding a frosting bag with a pointed tip. She saw me and breathed an audible sigh of relief. "Thank God! Career Services said they were sending somebody yesterday, but nobody showed up and they swore someone would show up today. You're the student from Pratt?"

"Yeah," I said. *Sure, why not.*

She handed me an apron. "What's your name?"

I don't know why, but I said, "Jana." I paused, and then realized how much better my new false identity could be with one simple change. "With an *h*," I added.

"Okay, Jahna-with-an-*h*," she said. "I'm Missoula. But everyone calls me Miss."

"Yes, ma'am," I said.

"*Miss*." She scanned all the tables. "I don't know where to start you. I only have this space till tomorrow and I have to get all these orders done by then. I've been working here round the clock all week, even sleeping here." She pointed to a futon in the corner of the room. I never realized gingerbread-house makers had to be such workaholics. I reconsidered it as a career and chose it as a sideline hobby instead of a lifetime pursuit.

"What can I do?" Could I put this experience on my future college applications?

"What's your major?"

"Food art," I said. God, Jahna was *so cool*.

"Fantastic," said Miss. "Can you do church duty first? That table over there needs its stained-glass windows painted in. I already drew the outlines, you just need to paint in the lines."

"Yes!" I squealed, and then realized: Jahna would never squeal. "I mean, whatever. Sure."

"Might be an all-nighter," said Miss.

"No problem," I said. Jahna was a starving student and could use the day's work for her train trip back home to Vermont for the holidays. Jahna was definitely from Vermont. But she might have done a junior year abroad in France, which is why she could be so effortlessly casual and sophisticated when she wasn't squealing like an idiot tween girl who just went to Disneyland for the first time. (Lily did that, and continues to do it every time she re-watches the video of her first time entering the Magic Kingdom.) Lily didn't have to worry about staying for the late night Jahna promised, because surely the real Pratt student would show up and relieve Jahna of duty, and they'd all have a laugh about missed communication, and ohmygod, I didn't realize *you* signed up for the job. Go ahead, you finish up, I'll just head home now.

Miss said, "Love your outfit, bee-tee-double-u." It took me a second to realize she meant "btw." "Is it vintage?"

I looked down at my school uniform. Fudgsicles. "Tee-why," said Jahna, for "ty." "And why-ee-ess yes!"

After that, I discovered Miss was not much of a talker. She was a doer. A frosting-spreading, gumdrop-placing, gingerbread-house-making work machine. The most I got out of her was that she was a freelance baker who'd gotten in over her head this year with custom gingerbread house orders. That was fine. I felt very Dash-reading-a-book about the whole experience, enjoying the feeling of aloneness while doing something I loved. An afternoon of decorating gingerbread houses was about as perfect a day as I could imagine.

The real Pratt student still hadn't shown up by

dinnertime, and I was hungry. I excused myself to get more Joe & Pat's pizza, and considered just skipping out on the rest of the job, because my family was probably starting to wonder where I was. I finished my pizza and bought some extra slices to bring back to Miss. The pizza would help cushion the blow when Jahna announced she had to quit for the night.

Miss was sitting slumped on the floor when I returned, exhausted. I handed her the pizza box. "You're an angel, Jahna," she said. "You literally saved me today." She wolfed down a slice and then said, "Wanna see the back room? That's where I really need the help. The real moneymakers are back there."

"*Oui!*" Jahna said. "*J'adore les moneymakers.*" Lily really needed to get home, but Jahna was extremely curious to know what was back there. Maybe Jahna should minor in French. It would open her up to so many diverse career opportunities after she graduated Pratt. She could study at Le Cordon Bleu. *Oui, oui, oui!*

Miss said, "You did such a beautiful job on the churches. You're not religious or anything, are you? Because I don't want you to be offended by what's in the back. The gingerbread cookies back there are, you know, rated X. Full-frontal men, if you know what I'm saying."

"No problem," I said. "It's not like I'm a virgin, ha ha!" Lily was the virgin. Jahna had had a mad love affair with her eighteenth-century French lit professor during her junior year abroad. It was all very secret, and Jahna regretted it

74

now because he was two decades older than her, but, wow, the sex had been *le amazing*. And the champagne and chocolate-dipped strawberries *après l'amour*.

Jahna may have been *le whatever* about what she saw in the back room, but Lily was wide-eyed shocked. "Rated X" was no exaggeration. My eyes had never, ever wanted to see gingerbread men and women in such various acts of . . .

"They're *Kama Sutra* cookies," said Miss. "All the major positions."

"I knew that," Jahna said, too quickly.

"They even have their own orgy den!" said Miss, laughing. She pointed to a completed gingerbread house decorated to look like a naughty gentlemen's club, with the words LIVE NUDES spelled out in white frosting on the roof, and Red Hots candies lining the sides to look like red lights.

Lily gulped, but Jahna said, "Awesome. Great work on the cutouts." I'm not going to lie. The gingerbread couples seemed very much in love, and they made me wish to experience the kind of passionate pleasure that was on their faces. Someday.

I couldn't wait to go home and find my phone, call Dash, and forget all the awkwardness lately. See him. Touch him. Sprinkle him in ginger and cinnamon and sugar, then smell him, and kiss him.

"Right?" said Miss. "It took me weeks to weld the cookie cutouts to just the right degrees of positions."

"You make it look so easy," said Jahna.

"*Thank* you! You've worked so hard all day. You deserve the truly fun task now." She handed me a bag of blue frosting, and then pointed to several trays of undecorated gingerbread females.

"Are these the girls who work in the gentlemen's club?" Jahna asked Miss knowingly.

"Hardly!" said Miss. "These girls are royalty." She lifted a piece of paper covering a drawing tacked to the wall behind the trays, showing voluptuous girls with long, braided hair doing unspeakable things. "Make 'em look like this. Princesses."

"Not Elsa and Anna!" Lily cried out. Lily wanted to go home so badly right now and never, *ever* watch *Frozen* again until these drawings had been obliterated from her memory.

"Right?" said Miss again. "I know, *bestsellers*!"

This was the time for Lily to bail, oh-bee-vee-ess. Obvs, I really missed my phone. And home. And Mommy. But then Miss said, "Want to taste Magic Mike?"

"Um, yes," said Jahna.

Miss winked at me. "This one's the special batch."

I took a bite of Magic Mike and, man, was that boy delicious. He tasted a little different than I expected.

"What's the special ingredient?" I asked.

"Right?" Miss said again.

Jahna probably knew what the special ingredient was, but Lily didn't. Jahna nodded knowingly again and said "Awesome" again.

I ate the cookie, and it was so good I had to have another, and then one more.

And then I was so relaxed and happy, I forgot the desire to leave. Suddenly I was really hungry for more pizza, and maybe some brownies, and it seemed to me that Elsa and Anna were really reaching their full artistic potential in Miss's gingerbread cookie drawings, and who was Jahna to deny them because Lily was such a Disney-loving virgin prude.

Jahna went to work.

Wednesday, December 17th

Jahna woke up on the futon when the sun burst through a hole in the papered windows of the store work space, but it was Lily who saw the clock on the wall and panicked. 11:15 a.m. FUDGE, FUDGE, FUDGE!

Miss was asleep on the floor.

I had no memory of falling asleep last night and no time to find out why I never made it home.

I bolted out the door and ran all the way to the ferry terminal. Knowing the level of crisis, I didn't even stop for a bagel. I didn't know what I feared more – how much trouble I was going to be in or that my family had gone totally *Home Alone* and hadn't even noticed I was gone.

The answer to both questions was on a TV monitor in the ferry waiting area. The TV was tuned to the NY1 channel. The sound was off, but on the screen I saw my picture, in which I was wearing my red pom-pom hat, followed by a cell phone video of a certain incident from last year. The headline running across the screen announced, "Teen Baby-Catcher Is Missing."

5
DASH

Put a Golden Ring on It

Wednesday, December 17th

It was about eight o'clock in the evening on Tuesday night when I received a text from Langston.

Is Lily with you?

I texted back: *No.*

Then he asked, *Do you know where she is?*

And I texted back: *No.*

Then I texted Lily. *Where are you?*

And I received the response: *If she hadn't left her phone behind, do you really think I'd be texting you?*

Which is how I realized that Lily was, like, *gone.*

Ordinarily, it would be no big deal if a teenager missed her curfew. It's practically a rite of passage. But Lily had never exhibited even a sprig of rumspringa, especially since she knew how much it would worry her grandfather if she didn't return home one night.

So we were worried.

I called around to our friends, but nobody had seen

her. Langston gave me periodic updates, and said his family phone tree had been activated.

Eleven o'clock, and still no word from her.

Midnight, and still no word from her.

Who's Edgar Thibaud? Langston texted.

Some jerk, I replied. Then added, *Why?*

Just wondering if he would know where Lily was.

Why?

No reason.

That seemed weird. I had no idea that Edgar Thibaud and Lily were still in contact – but that was certainly what Langston's question implied.

I filed that away.

12:30 – no word.

1:00 – no word.

It was hard to sleep. I dozed on and off, waking up every hour to get word from Langston.

2:00 – no word.

3:00 – police notified.

4:00 – calling around to hospitals.

5:00 – no word.

6:00 – A sighting! Staten Island.

6:01 – I text to Langston: *So we're going to Staten Island, right?*

6:01:30 – *Right.*

As I got dressed – as I explained to my sleeping mother why I had to skip school today, as I left the apartment and headed downtown to catch the ferry – all I could think was, *This has to be my fault.* A better boyfriend would have prevented his girlfriend from disappearing. A better boyfriend wouldn't have given his girlfriend any reason to disappear. He wouldn't have burned down her Christmas party. He would've known how to read her even if she was acting unreadable.

Where are you, Lily? I kept thinking.

"It's all my fault."

Langston did not look happy to be telling me this. He also looked like he felt he had to.

"Why do you say that?" I asked. We were standing on the deck of the Staten Island Ferry, even though it was really too cold and too early to be standing on the deck. The boat was pushing away from the dock, and our own batteries were just starting to get out of park. While there were plenty of people who'd gotten off in Manhattan to head to their skyscraper jobs, there weren't that many people heading toward Staten Island at this hour. We were getting everything backwards.

At first I didn't think Langston was going to answer me – enough time went by that I started to wonder if we'd actually said anything at all, or if it was just my Lily-is-gone delirium that was inducing imaginary conversations. But then Langston lifted his right hand and showed me a gold ring he was wearing on his pinky.

"Benny and I decided to start taking what we have

seriously. Which means moving in together. And moving in together means moving out of the building I've been living in most of my life. I told Lily about it yesterday, and she didn't take it well. I knew she wouldn't . . . but I guess I'd hoped that I'd be wrong. That she'd understand. But why would she understand?"

"Are you saying that she couldn't understand because she isn't, you know, in the kind of lasting relationship that, say, you and Benny are in?"

Langston shook his head. "Not everything I say is a rebuke to you, you know."

"No. Maybe it's just a buke. And then when you repeat it in twenty minutes, *that* will be the rebuke."

Langston whistled a note and looked out over the water, as if maybe the Statue of Liberty was going to sympathize with him for being stuck with me.

"The funny thing," he said, still facing the bay, "is that Lily's the only person I know who's as high-strung as you are. *Thinking* is your favorite thing to do, isn't it? Sometimes it's endearing, but sometimes it's completely exhausting."

It wasn't like Langston to concede that Lily and I had anything in common. So I decided to take this as a compliment. And at the same time, I decided not to press the point.

I followed Langston's glance and stared out at the water, too. At Ellis Island. At the receding giants sitting on the downtown shore. Anyone who's lived in Manhattan all his life always feels torn whenever he leaves it. There's the satisfaction of breaking free, for a time. But that's balanced heavily by the feeling of leaving your whole life behind, and to see it from a distance.

I wanted Lily to be there next to me. I knew that made no sense, since if she'd been next to me I wouldn't have been looking for her – but at the same time, it felt like perfect sense. She was the person I wanted to share life with the most, and it was the moments of noticing that made me feel this most acutely.

I couldn't tell if Langston was thinking of Benny, or of Lily, or if he wasn't thinking of anyone at all. I wasn't sharing this with Lily, but I was sharing it with him. Or at least I knew I would be sharing it with him if we kept talking, if we bridged my experience of the moment and his experience of the moment.

"You want to hear something strange?" I said, my voice a little louder to make headway against the wind. "This is the first time I've ever taken the Staten Island Ferry. I always meant to, but it was never a priority. I took a ferry to see the Statue of Liberty on a field trip in, like, fifth grade – but other than that, I've stayed away from the water."

"I once dated a boy in Staten Island," Langston replied. "I met his parents on the first date. And the second date. And the third. So I tend to associate the borough with guys who don't particularly want to get away from their families. Unfortunately, by the time the fourth date came around, *I* wanted to get away from his family."

"When you broke up with him, did you do something

drastic? Like, say, burn down their Christmas tree?"

Langston didn't smile. "What kind of madman would do that?"

"A madman in love?"

Now he smiled ... a little. "That, sir, is a very interesting point."

"We always torch the ones we love –"

"– the ones we shouldn't torch at all."

"Precisely."

Full stop. More wind. More wake. The Statue of Liberty behind us now, no longer greeting us, but instead looking like we'd left her to fend for herself, waiting for the guy she'd met on the Internet whose first words to her would be, "You looked smaller in your profile pic."

Langston turned to look at the island we were approaching. "The answer is: I didn't burn down his tree. Or his house. Or his heart. I just stopped talking to him. I disappeared back into Manhattan. I imagine he's found a nice boy from the neighborhood, and their families have dinner together every Sunday at five."

I couldn't help myself – I had to ask, "Is that a family trait? Disappearing?"

Now he turned back to me. "Yes. But you have to understand – Lily's not like the rest of us. Lily's the best we've got."

"I hope you don't mind if I agree with that point. Although she *does* seem to have disappeared."

Staten Island was clear to us now, its houses and hills

a contrast to the land we'd left. I'd thought it would take longer to get there. I had to remind myself that we were still in the same city. If our information was correct, Lily was that much closer. But she was still gone.

"It's all my fault," I found myself saying to Langston.

He leaned on the railing, put his hands in his coat pockets. "Why do you say that?"

"I haven't been able to reach her. And if I can't reach her, there's no way to keep her from being lost."

The blast of a horn drowned out any possible response. The ferry sputtered, as if it was having second thoughts. Then it pulled into the dock.

"Come on," Langston said.

I followed him down the plank, into the terminal. When we got to the door leading to the street, I asked him, "What now?"

"I honestly have no idea."

This was not what I wanted to hear. I imagined he'd have a serious plan, involving the triangulation of coordinates, the canvassing of neighborhoods, the cross-examining of samaritans.

"Well, where was she last seen?" I asked.

"By my exile uncle at his garage. But that was many hours ago. And Staten Island is much bigger than you think it is. Most people here have cars."

"Cars?"

"Seriously. Cars."

"Then what should we do? Take a cab around? Look

for her?"

"I'm not sure. I mean, it would be one thing if there were favorite places we could check, or if we had some idea what she was doing here. But I'm not sure where she'd go. And it doesn't seem like it would be all that helpful for us to split up and wander around. We'll only get lost ourselves."

"So what are we doing here?"

"Trying to make ourselves feel better. That's what guys do."

I sighed. The more I thought about it, the stupider it seemed to wander around Staten Island in search of a girl. It wasn't just a matter of pinpointing the needle – we couldn't even find the right haystack.

"She's going to come back," Langston continued. "And when she does, it's going to be on the ferry. So maybe we should ride it until she comes on board. We'll find her then."

"But what if she's been abducted? What if she needs our help?"

"When was the last time you got your detective license renewed, Sherlock? I don't think we're the best hounds to sniff out this particular Baskerville. And every brotherly instinct in my body is telling me that Lily hasn't been teen-napped. I think she went for a wander. I don't know if she wants to be found, but I also think it will mean something to her to know we were trying to find her. So let's carry on."

An announcement was made: The ferry was about to

leave again.

"All aboard," I said.

We didn't talk for three stretches across the bay. By the fourth go-round, the novelty of the windy deck had worn off, and we'd found ourselves a bench inside. At first I occupied myself by looking at our fellow travelers. When the boat was heading to Manhattan, it was full of people crowded into their own routines, like they had timed their newspaper reading to every league traveled, their cruller consumption paced so the last crumb was licked just as it was time to stand and leave. On the trip back to Staten Island, the people looked more like me and Langston – the non-commuters, temporarily unmoored and slightly unnerved. There was one man in his fifties who rode back and forth with us, reading a Jonathan Franzen novel at a pace usually reserved for glaciers and drunk children. At one point he looked up as I was looking over, and I forswore eye contact as quickly as I could . . . which was still too late. I was afraid to aggressively people-watch after that.

I found myself staring instead at the ring Langston was wearing. I thought about him and Benny moving in together, taking that step. Langston caught me staring and raised an eyebrow.

"How did you know?" I asked him. "I mean, what told you that you were ready to make that leap?"

I half expected him to tell me it was none of my business, or that there wasn't any way for me to understand. But instead he looked at me seriously and said, "I don't think it's a matter of ready – I mean, not in an all-the-way sense. You're never completely ready – you just get to the point where you're ready enough. With us, we didn't decide to move in together – we just slept over at one another's places enough that we'd practically moved in together, and then realized it would be much more practical to actually do it."

"But do you love him? I mean – *rings.*"

Langston smiled and started to play with the ring, rotating it back and forth on his pinky as if to prove that it wasn't coming off.

"Of course I love him. And I might even love him enough to stop being so afraid of it. That's what we have to find out. And this is the way to find out – to wake up each morning and start each day together, to be the continuity for each other even when everything else is discontinuous or fickle or cruel. I know in my heart that I can live without him and I know in my heart that I don't want to – that's a good place to start, right?"

I agreed . . . and wanted to know more. "But how do you get there? How do you get to that point?"

Langston let go of the ring, leaned back in his seat. "Are you talking about you and Lily?"

"I guess."

"You *guess*?"

"I mean, yes. I mean . . . I feel we could have that, you know? In some way. At some point. But every time we get close to it, we get shy. I don't mean with each other. It's more like we get shy with ourselves. I don't think about me and Lily being good enough together – I think about whether I'm good enough for Lily. I try to be a bright spot. And sometimes with the two of us, it *is* bright. But a lot of the time, I'm just a spot. It all feels so big, and I'm just a spot."

"And only intermittently bright."

"Gee, thanks."

"No – that's cool. Too much brightness is damn hard to look at."

This wasn't a comfort. This wasn't anything, really. I didn't even know what I was saying anymore. I was restless. Talking about Lily usually made me feel as if she was there in some way, in the same way that thinking about her made her feel closer. But that wasn't working now.

"This is pointless," I said.

"What?"

It frustrated me that I had to explain – didn't he feel it, too? "Waiting here. Talking. Thinking. It all feels pointless. She's going to do what she wants to do, and she'll come home when she wants to come home, and ultimately she'll be with me if she wants to be with me."

"And you want to be with her?"

"*Yes.*"

"Does she know that?"

"What do *you* think?"

"I don't know."

Oh great, I thought. *That is hardly reassuring.* And then I felt stupid for wanting reassurance when I didn't feel I deserved it.

Langston went on. "It's the paradox, isn't it? The people you know the most, the people you love the most – you're also going to feel the parts of them you don't know the most. I can tell you the cereal Benny eats, the pair of socks that's his favorite, the part of a movie – any movie – that will make him cry. The way he knots a tie. The nicknames he has for each of his cousins. The third-worst heartbreak he ever had. And the seventh. And the tenth, which shouldn't even count. But there are times when he will fall into this deep incomprehensibility, when he will like something or need something or not need something that I can't believe he'd like or need or not need, and I will be frightened that I have gotten every single thing about him wrong, including us."

"Then what do you do?" I asked. I really, really wanted to know. There wasn't anyone else to tell me. None of my friends had reached that point. And my parents had reached that point, then fell from it hard.

"I wait," Langston said. "I remind myself that I don't need to know everything, that there will always be essential rooms within us that will be unknown. I loosen my idea of him, and he becomes recognizable again."

"It's not that Lily's unrecognizable. It's just that she's . . . not there as much."

Langston sighed. "Well, there's been a lot going on."

"I know that. Really, I do."

"I didn't say that to make you feel bad. I actually said

90

that to make you feel better."

"I'm not sure you were successful at either."

"Look, I'm worried, too. When Benny and I made our decision, the hardest part was imagining how it would leave Lily. I almost said no – I honestly wasn't sure I could do it. But Benny – Benny asked me a really good question: *Who exactly are you helping here?* Which means: Lily's going to need to find her own way, and she's going to need to grow up beyond our apartment and our family. I'm not going to like it when she makes her own way, in the same way that I'm sure she's not liking the fact that I'm making my own way. But if we don't, we'll stay in the same place our whole lives."

I had enough distance from the conversation to know that the idea of Lily going her own way was not an indictment of the idea of her staying with me. I knew that Langston was talking about him and her, not me and anyone.

"I should go to school," I said to Langston.

I wanted him to argue and I didn't want him to argue.

"That's probably a good idea," he said. "This job doesn't require four eyes. And when I find Lily, I will be sure to convey your efforts."

This was the difference the day had made: Before, I would have thought this was sarcasm. Now I knew it was sincere.

How crazy would it be, to have won over Lily's brother but to have lost Lily?

I tried to prevent myself from thinking about that.

I wasn't very successful.

The next time we docked in Battery Park, I disembarked. As the ferry pulled away again, I spotted Langston on the deck.

I nodded to him.

He nodded back.

Then the ferry was gone, and all that was left was waves.

Another person might have skipped out on school. He might have taken the day off, gone back to bed. But I wanted the distraction of people talking about winter break plans. I wanted the last round of classes, the last round of time killing.

Or at least that's what I told myself I wanted. But once I got there, I couldn't really get there. I kept checking my phone. Word of Lily's disappearance had hit the news, and so many people were using me as an outlet for their concern. Friends asking if they could help. Friends asking if I wanted to talk. Friends wondering where she'd gone, as if I was keeping it a secret, but would tell them, just them, nobody else but them.

My father called.

How strange for him to be concerned, I thought.

But when I picked up – fool, I! – I found that his call had nothing to do with Lily.

"Leeza just wanted me to confirm that you'll be with us for Christmas," he said. "She has to confirm the reservation, and has been on my case about the head count."

This was the first time I'd heard of the reservation, or the plans.

"Dad, I have no idea what you're talking about," I told him. "And can't you just text me like everyone else's parents do?"

"I'm sure I told you. Didn't I?"

"Maybe you were going to before you ran away from Lily's party?"

I knew I was crossing the line, but I didn't care. For once, I wanted to be the one making the lines.

"Watch your tone, Dash."

"I got it from you, Dad," I replied.

Then I hung up.

It should have felt good, but it didn't feel good. It wasn't going to end anything. It was only going to piss him off more.

My girlfriend is missing, I should have been able to tell him.

What can I do to help? he should have been able to ask.

But we were both so fundamentally incapable.

At least I'd learned the lesson that friends can make up for the failings of your family. Between third and fourth period, Sofia and Boomer stopped me in the halls, and I was grateful for it.

"We heard the news," Sofia said. "Is there anything we can do?"

"If you want," Boomer offered, "I can talk to that girl Amber in my chem class and see if she can put out an alert."

"I don't think it works that way," Sofia said. "But it's a

93

nice thought."

"It's my pleasure," Boomer said. Then he looked at me and his face fell. "Not that I'm taking any pleasure in this. I'm not, I swear."

"I'm sure she'll be back soon," I assured him. "I think she just needed some space."

"So maybe she's at the planetarium!"

"I see your logic there, my friend. I'll text her brother and ask him to check."

This made Boomer happy. Then, worried again that he seemed too happy, he tried to get more serious again. It wasn't a look he wore well. Finally he said, "It's time for English – I better get going!" and hopped down the hall.

Sofia turned and watched him go. I begrudgingly admitted to myself that it was sweet, the way she did it.

I wondered if I did the same thing with Lily. And then I wondered if it was the kind of thing you'd even notice when you were doing it, or if it was one of those breathing-level things you did without realizing.

"She went to Staten Island," I told Sofia. "I tried to find her, but I didn't make it beyond the ferry."

"Most people don't," Sofia consoled. "Unless they live in Staten Island."

I had once been Sofia's boyfriend. Now I wanted to ask her if I'd been a good one, if even though she and I hadn't worked out, she believed that I could work out with someone. I just couldn't find a way to ask the question.

But Sofia must have known anyway. Because she looked

at me and said, "Wherever she is, whatever she's doing – it's not about you. It's about her. And you have to let it be about her. Sometimes we don't want to be found right away. If we step away, it's because we need to be found on our own terms."

"You didn't disappear," I pointed out.

"Maybe I did," she replied. "Maybe I do."

The bell rang then.

"She's not leaving you," Sofia told me before she went. "If she was leaving you, you'd know."

But I wasn't sure what I knew. Or what I noticed.

Finally, a little before noon, Langston texted.

Found her. Safe and sound.

I knew she didn't have her phone yet, unless Langston had brought it with him. (I hadn't thought to ask.) But I texted her right away anyway, figuring she'd get the message whenever she got back home.

Welcome back, I said. *I missed you.*

Then I waited for her reply.

6
LILY

Geese a-Twerking

Wednesday, December 17th

I don't know why, but I wasn't at all surprised when I stepped onto the boat and saw my brother already on it, waiting for me.

Langston pulled me to him for a hug, but it was equal parts throttle. "Don't *ever* give us a scare like that again," he said.

As the ferry pulled out from the dock, returning us to Manhattan, my brother got our parents on his phone for a FaceTime call.

"Where were you?" Mom shrieked. She looked like she hadn't slept all night.

"I needed a time-out," I said. I'm not proud to report I then went into full lying mode. I don't know what it is about being a teenager, but lying seems to be necessitated with the hormonal territory. All these people in your life expecting you to act like an adult, and then getting mad when you take a stab at independence. "I went to Uncle Rocco's panic room. I fell asleep and it was so dark in there, I didn't wake up till half an hour ago. Sorry to have worried you."

There was precedent for the lie. On many an annual trip to Staten Island to visit the family burial plots, I was known to take time-outs from family fights with Uncle Rocco and hide in the Cold War bunker built into a secret basement at his auto body shop, two blocks away from the cemetery.

What was I supposed to say? *I'm feeling lost and confused and didn't feel like going to school, so I went to Staten Island, and took on a new identity there. Still with me? Jahna – you'd like her, she's much cooler than me – got lured into an enchanting gingerbread-house-making operation that turned a little strange after eating a few Magic Mike cookies. Then Jahna became a naughty, Frozen-themed gingerbread-decorating machine who passed out from whatever secret ingredient made Mike's cookies so magical, and she woke up as boring old Lily again less than an hour ago.*

The lie would merely relegate me to "Lily's being an oddball again and should we put her back into therapy?" territory. The truth would probably send me immediately to a rehab facility.

"Don't ever, ever do that again," said Dad. "I think you aged us a decade last night."

I looked at my mom's face, and I could see her anger and fatigue, but I also sensed something else: calm. "I was worried," Mom said. "But somehow I trusted you were okay. I felt it. When my mother died, and when my cousin Lawrence was in that terrible car accident, when Grandpa fell, I knew before I even got the calls that something was terribly wrong. I didn't have that instinct last night. As panicked as I was, I felt sure you were fine, wherever you were."

It probably wasn't the time to nitpick, but I did anyway. "Do we not think alerting NY1 wasn't a little over the top?" I said.

Dad said, "They have a soft spot for you. They got a sweet ratings spike from the baby-catching incident."

I pointed out, "That's not a soft spot. That's opportunism."

Mom said, "We waited until sunrise, but when we still hadn't heard from you, we thought alerting them might smoke you out from wherever you were hiding. And we were right. Uncle Rocco saw the report, and called to say he'd seen you on the island yesterday."

"Too much," I said.

"I hardly think you're in a position to criticize," said Mom.

"We'll talk about it when you get home," said Dad. "Family meeting."

I said, "I'm sorry. Really."

Their faces disappeared from Langston's phone as he ended the call. Langston said, "I've ridden this ferry back and forth five times, waiting for you."

It was like he wanted me to say, "Thanks." I didn't. I was so mad at him for being ready to move out of our family home. I wanted to be happy for his happiness with Benny, but I was so sad for me. They were ready. I wasn't.

When I didn't say anything, Langston added, "Dash came with me for the first few ferry trips. He was really worried, too."

"Oh," was all I said. Dash's so-called worry was just like Dash's Christmas tree gift. He acted like he wanted to be there for me, and then he prematurely abandoned ship. Cold, impassable. Why did he have to be so handsome and caring, but not in love?

Dash was such a complication in my life. I had more pressing concerns. Like, where would I be sent to live if my family home was being broken apart?

"He's a decent guy," said Langston, causing my head to do a near-360-degree headspin of shock.

"So you like Dash now?" I said, incredulous.

"I *tolerate* Dash now," said Langston.

Everything I knew about the world was spun on its axis, and I was confused, and scared, but admittedly intrigued by the mystery and excitement of the new directions my life could possibly be going in. I said, "I *tolerate* that you and Benny might be happy together in your new apartment that I don't approve of but will support anyway."

"That's how I feel about you dating Dash." Pause. "He really cares about you."

I thought, *That's the problem.* I love. Dash cares. It hurt.

"Then why isn't he here now?" I said.

"He had to get to school. Apparently Dash takes school more seriously than you have the last couple days." My brother looked at me slyly and then asked, "So where were you, really?"

"At a gingerbread-house-making orgy."

Langston said, "Sarcasm doesn't become you, Lily. If you don't want to tell me, just don't."

We returned home as Mom and Dad were frantically preparing to leave for a weeklong trip to Connecticut, for Dad's school's holiday party and to close out the academic semester at his job. They were also going so that Mom could see and experience the headmaster's quarters for herself, with the expectation that they might move to the boarding school's grounds in the new year.

The family meeting was over in a New York minute.

Academic punishment: Because I'd skipped school, the school's policy was that I wouldn't be allowed to make up the work from the two days of school I'd missed, and my grades would reflect the consequences. Also, I was suspended for the last two days of school till the holiday, which I didn't understand at all, because that "punishment" was more like a present. Two more days off! So what if I couldn't make up the schoolwork? I could use that time to bake cookies and walk dogs and make Christmas presents, and do lots more interesting stuff than being at school.

Parental punishment: Except for dog-walking duties, I was grounded till Christmas.

I've never been grounded before. I didn't even know what it meant, technically. I didn't think my parents did either, because they issued the proclamation just before leaving town, effectively rendering their punishment unenforceable. (I didn't bring up that small point.)

Honestly, I didn't feel that bad about giving my parents a sleepless night. I was a Manhattan girl. The Connecticut-considering deserters deserved the worry.

Grandpa, however, didn't. He said, "I'm staying at my sister's for a while. Too much commotion here. You don't have to bother with taking me to doctor appointments anymore."

"I like doing that, Grandpa!" I said.

He used his cane to lift the bottom of his pant leg, revealing a bruise on his shin. "See that?" he asked me, pointing to it with his cane.

"What happened?" I asked.

"You didn't show up for your volunteer shift at the rehab center is what happened! Sadie in room 506 was so angry not to have you reading to her today that she actually kicked me."

"Sorry, Grandpa."

"And I lost big guessing at *Wheel of Fortune* without my good luck charm sitting beside me."

"Sorry, Grandpa."

"I *hate Wheel of Fortune*! The only thing that makes it tolerable to watch with all those old fuddy-duddies is having you there to watch it with us."

"Sorry, Grandpa."

What kind of monster was I?

Grandpa didn't look me in the eyes. "You're grounded," was all he said. Then he stood up, grabbed on to his cane, and hobbled away from me.

Seeing his back turn on me was the worst punishment I could have imagined. The one that tore my heart.

When I was reunited with my phone in the new temporary prison that was my room, I saw the text from Dash. *Welcome back. I missed you.*

I missed you, too, I answered.

I fell asleep clutching my phone, with my dog and Grandpa's cat keeping me warm. I wished the warmth had come from Dash-in-the-flesh holding me tight, and not Dash texting loud, but saying nothing.

Thursday, December 18th

Edgar Thibaud was sitting at his usual table in Tompkins Square Park when I walked by with that day's collection of dogs. He was playing chess with the park champion, an older gentleman named Cyril who has Rastafarian dreadlocks, matted with strands of gray hair, and who wears a beret he won off Edgar during a tournament last spring.

Edgar said, "'sup, Lily? Where've ya been? Haven't seen you here or at the senior center this week."

"The park's not the same without you and your dogs," said Cyril, contemplating a row of rooks on the chessboard.

"Smells better without those poop machines, though,"

said Edgar. He eyed Boris accusingly. "Yeah, I'm looking at you, buddy."

I never know with Edgar whether I want to strangle him or try to rehabilitate him.

"Don't speak to my dog rudely, please," I told Edgar. Boris barked in agreement.

"Are you coming to my party tonight?" Edgar asked me.

"What party?" I asked.

"My annual Christmas sweater party."

"You have an annual Christmas sweater party?"

"Now I do. Parents are in Hong Kong, house to myself, Christmas sweater collection just returned from dry cleaners. A party's in order."

"Can I bring Dash?" I asked Edgar.

"Do you have to?"

"Kind of."

Edgar sighed. "I guess. Bring whomever you want. BYOB."

"What's BYOB?" I asked.

"Bring Your Own Boob!" said Cyril with a laugh.

"Believe me, she will," said Edgar. "The boob's name is Dash. But tell him to bring his own beer."

"I don't think Dash drinks beer."

"Of course he doesn't. God forbid he actually have fun sometime."

"She was such a good girl before she met you," Langston told Dash, who'd come to my house to pick me up for the

103

party. I was grounded, but Langston was in charge during my parents' absence. Not only was there a solid tradition of everything going wrong when Langston was in charge, but Langston also owed me for all the years when he was in high school and I covered for him when he broke curfew or snuck in boyfriends to spend the night.

"Says the man who suggested the red notebook last Christmas, leading Lily on her path to fallen woman," said Dash.

Langston looked at me and pointed at Dash. "Now *that* is quality sarcasm." He looked at Dash. "Have her home by midnight and spend the night if you want to."

Dash's and my faces both reddened, and we hastened out the door. "Take good care of Boris," I said to my brother.

Once we were down on the street, Dash took my hand in his and we began walking. "So, Edgar Thibaud?" he said. "Seriously?" He didn't say, *Because I had better plans. Because tonight is the night I was going to finally surprise you with a date to see* Corgi & Bess. *I rented the whole theater out just for us, and our center seats are covered in rose petals, and there's a donut tower cake with chocolate dripping down its sides there that I ordered for just us to enjoy. Just us! The ENTIRE donut cake!*

I said, "Edgar has to work at Grandpa's senior center. I see him in the park all the time when I'm dog walking. He practically lives there."

"You're friends?"

"I guess?" I said.

"I'm confused why you never mentioned it." He didn't say, *I'm outraged you never mentioned your friendship with Edgar! It makes me CRAZY to think of you hanging out with him. Everyone knows Edgar Thibaud is a world class dawg in designer argyle, and I might have to, like, challenge him to a duel for your affection!*

"Does it matter?" I asked. *Please. Let it matter!*

Dash shrugged. "Guess not." Boys never say what you want them to. It's probably the only lesson I've learned in life. "But we could go to your aunt's instead. Mrs. Basil E. texted me to invite us to come over for dinner and play Cards Against Humanity after with her and Grandpa and –"

"You text with my great-aunt?"

"Yes. Does it matter?"

I shrugged. "Guess not." Then: "Cards Against Humanity is such a rude game." Mrs. Basil E. had never invited me to play that game with her before.

"I know. That's why I love it."

Finally. Good Lily was behind me.

Hello, Naughty Lily. You're *fun*.

Naughty Lily wore a short black skirt with black leggings and thigh-high black boots, and a cropped – yes, *cropped* – Christmas sweater, red and gold and green with two auspiciously placed glitter ornament decorations sewn across the very tight chest.

"Did Langston see you wearing that?" Dash asked when

I took my coat off, right after he rang the doorbell to Edgar Thibaud's townhouse.

"Do you like it?" I asked, trying to sound sexy, but sounding more desperately shrill. (Naughty Lily would need more practice to acquire sexy voice tones. Her innate Shrilly refuses to die.)

"I guess I'm happy you're finally feeling the Christmas spirit," said Dash.

"What's your sweater?" I asked him.

He opened his coat, revealing ... a plain green polo sweater with a white oxford shirt peeking out from the collar.

"That's not really a Christmas sweater," I said.

"You're not looking carefully enough." He pulled the oxford collar out from its tuck in the sweater's neck. I looked more closely and saw a quote from *A Christmas Carol* written in alternating red and gold ink in Dash's handwriting across the bottom edge of the collar. Marley was dead: to begin with.

The door opened as my face peered into Dash's neck. From the other side of the door, Edgar announced, "Lovebirds PDA'ing already? The eggnog hasn't even been served yet."

Dash pulled away from me and closed his coat. "I don't PDA, Edgar."

Edgar winked at Dash. "Of course you don't. Welcome, party animal." He eyed me up and down and said, "Loving your sweater, Lillers."

Edgar wore a sweater picturing Jesus wearing a birthday hat in the shape of a slice of upside-down pepperoni pizza and the words BIRTHDAY BOY written across the Chosen One's chest, which Edgar had paired with pink and gray argyle pants and black and white saddle shoes. It's impossible to overstate how grossly mismatched his outfit was, kind of like Edgar in his own house.

His parents are, like, the 1 percent of the 1 percent, hedge fund managers with bazillions of bucks and no time to spend on their son. Mrs. Basil E. also lives in a townhouse, but hers is musty and arty and sort of falling apart. Very welcoming. Edgar's is like an architectural magazine showpiece, with severe, minimalist furniture and million-dollar pieces of art on the walls. Very intimidating and cold.

"'Lillers'?" Dash whispered in my ear as we walked up the marble stairs to the second level. "Please."

"Your friends arrived ahead of you," said Edgar. "Fun kids. They've already hit the eggnog, as you can see."

And there in the center of the drawing room were Boomer and Sofia, wearing matching Christmas goose sweaters, dirty-dancing as a hip-hop song blasted from invisible speakers. They were laughing and kissing as they butt-shimmied nearly to the ground, then knocked butts, their ease and joy in each other readily apparent. I wished Dash and I could be like them. Twerking for the sake of the twerk, and not caring who watched, because they were too wrapped up – literally – in each other.

"Eggnog?" Edgar asked Dash. "It's spiked with Father's

vintage Jack Daniel's Sinatra Century Limited Edition."

"Yes, please!" said Naughty Lily. I looked at my Young Blue Eyes – Dashiell – hoping we could imbibe some naughtiness together. Clink our frothy glasses and then share a Sinatra Century Limited Edition-flavored kiss. Or twenty.

"No thank you," said Dash. Shoo be do be DARN.

In a baby voice, Edgar asked Dash, "Would wittle boy wike some pwain yogurt instead?"

Dash touched the side of his nose and asked Edgar, "Jack Frost nipping at your nose?"

His nose wasn't running that I could tell, but Edgar fell for the bait and pulled a handkerchief from his argyle pants pocket and blew into it. Then he said, "You guys in for Spin the Dreidel later? Winners get to make out in my parents' bedroom, under the Motherwell. Ha ha, get it?"

Our host went to find his eggnog decanter as Dash and I inspected the room. The party was in full swing, yes – but there were only about a dozen people there, a totally mismatched collection of people. Me, Dash, twerking Boomer and Sofia, Cyril doing the hustle with Isabella Fontana, a retired cookbook editor who's one of my dog-walking clients and really should have been more mindful of her recent hip replacement surgery, and some samba-dancing, drunk Korean party kids whom I recognized from Edgar's ramen-emergency FaceTime call, which had precipitated my soul-searching journey to Staten Island. The partygoers ranged in age from about seventeen to seventy, and wore sweaters with snowmen, angels, Santas, elves, reindeer, and Christmas cats. Edgar stood against the wall, in front of the party table with an ice sculpture of two kissing geese as its centerpiece, admiring the odd collection of mismatched people and their mismatched sweaters. He'd never looked more alone to me than in his own house. A prince with no kingdom.

"I'd rather go somewhere private," said Dash to me. "Where we could talk. I have something important to tell you."

That's when I knew. Dash was going to break up with me. He was finally going to break our awkward impasse.

"Let's dance?" I asked him, wanting to hold on to him one last time.

An R&B version of "Let It Snow" started playing, as the singer crooned, *Ohhhh, come over here and help me trim the tree / I wanna wrap you up.*

"Please?" I asked Dash. I wanted to remember this last moment, wrapped up in him.

He stood so tall and stiff, uncomfortable. But then Boomer and Sofia came over and led us to the center of the room. They began a slow dance, and then, following their lead, Dash placed his arms around my waist, and I placed mine on his shoulders, and we danced.

I was giddy. I knew Dash hated it, and I loved him for going along with it anyway. My heart actually surged with joy as I pressed my body closer to his, and I thought I could feel his heart beating against mine. He felt so good, and I never wanted to let go. I had to tell him I loved him – just take the risk, just get over my insecurities and doubts about the impossibility of it all – before it was too late.

"I have something to tell you," I whispered into Dash's ear.

"I have something to tell you, too," he said.

I had to tell him. I had to.

And just as I was about to, I saw Dash make a momentary glance at twerking Sofia, giving her the look I always wished he'd direct at me. Pure want. I try not to be jealous of effortlessly gorgeous Sofia and the fact that she and Dash used to be a couple; I don't always succeed.

So I said it first. "I think we should break up."

7
DASH

Swan Song

Thursday, December 18th

And I said, "No."

Wednesday, December 17th

When I didn't hear back from Lily after her mysterious return from Staten Island, I went back over all the texts I'd exchanged with Langston, and one name popped out:

Edgar Thibaud.

Why had Langston asked me about him?

What was he to Lily?

I knew they had an unsavory history. I knew he'd tried to hijack her affections when my own affections for her had been new.

Most of all, I knew he was King Asshole.

I suppose I could have asked Langston – but our newfound respect was only a day old, and I didn't particularly want to test it.

Lily had let slip at some point that Thibaud had been

sentenced to community service at the place where her grandfather had gone for rehab. So after school, I decided to go to the source.

Thursday, December 18th

"What do you mean, *no*?" Lily asked. "What do you care?"

She tried to pull away.

I held on.

Wednesday, December 17th

Thibaud had a way of making the professionals as forgetful as their patients. Every nurse had a different answer when I asked for his whereabouts. None of the answers were correct.

Finally a smirking Sadie with a bright pink walking stick took pity on me.

"You looking for the troublemaker?" she rasped.

I had no doubt I was, and told her so.

"Well then, look in the custodian's closet between 36A and 36B. He's usually dodging work there. But be careful — he's a wobbly pair of dentures, that one. Don't let him out if you don't want him giving you the slip."

The way Smirking Sadie said this, she almost sounded jilted.

I skirted around the wheelchairs, and a whole lot of people watching *Wheel of Fortune*, to find the closet she was talking about. Once I got there, I didn't know whether to knock. Then I heard the sounds coming from inside and knew it had to be Thibaud.

I plunged in.

What I saw was disturbing in the extreme. Thibaud was watching porn on his phone, featuring two women, a horse, and a man who looked uncannily like Donald Trump. At the same time, he was smoking a cigarette, tipping the ashes down into a bedpan. His feet were on the custodian's desk.

"Surely this breaks a limit for simultaneous vices!" I announced in my most authoritarian tone. Thibaud started, jumping up and switching off his phone.

"What the –!" he yelled. Then he saw it was me, and didn't seem quite as freaked out. "Oh. Dash. What, did you think your missing girlfriend was in here with me?"

I didn't like his insinuation, and told him so. Then I added, "Plus, she's no longer missing."

"Have you seen her?" he challenged. Then, before I could bluff, he extinguished his cigarette in the bedpan and said, "I thought not."

Before I could edgewise a word into his skull, he opened the door and pushed out into the hallway. I followed on his heels.

"Oh no, you don't," I said. But he did, pushing into the TV room, completely ignoring me.

"Does anybody need anything?" he asked the old people there.

"A vowel! I need a vowel!" a blue-haired lady cried out, gesturing to the TV.

| L | | | | | A | | | R |, the screen said.

"Love caster!" the blue-haired lady trilled.

"Love master!" a man in a wheelchair called out.

"Love washer!" a man in gray corduroy called out.

The man in the wheelchair was offended. "What the hell's a *love washer*?"

"Heh heh," the corduroy man laughed. "You don't remember, do you?"

"Why are you texting Lily?" I asked Thibaud. "What is she to you?"

"Why are you asking me and not her?" he shot back.

L N AN R

"Long canter!" the blue-haired lady shrieked.

"Lone cantor!" the man in the wheelchair insisted.

"Lone manger!" the corduroy man coughed.

Thibaud turned on me and spat, "You are a miserable excuse for a boyfriend! You are, like, the safety school of boyfriends. You are the beige of boyfriends. You are the *plain yogurt* of boyfriends."

"Did Lily tell you that?"

"Of course!" he replied with a bright smile.

Thursday, December 18th

I couldn't believe she'd said it. And I couldn't believe she'd meant it.

I think we should break up.

I was confused.

I was upset.

I was *angry*.

"You're getting it wrong," I told her. "You're getting *everything wrong*."

Wednesday, December 17th

Thibaud's smile was too bright. I knew he was lying.

"Leave her alone!" I warned. "Just leave Lily alone."

"Or what? You'll strangle me with your vocabulary? You'll punch me with your mighty wit?"

The room had fallen deathly silent. I looked at the screen.

`L U N G` `C A N C   R`

Jesus.

"Challenge him to a duel!" the man in the wheelchair groused at me.

"Yeah!" the corduroy man choked out. "Nail that weasly bastard. He always steals my goddamn applesauce!"

"Fine," I told them. Then I turned to Thibaud and said, "I challenge you to a duel."

Thursday, December 18th

"How can you say that?" Lily yelled. Everyone was watching us. Then, nonsensically, she added, *"That's not even a Christmas sweater!"*

Wednesday, December 17th

"And how do you suggest we duel?" Thibaud said, unimpressed.

I looked back to the old men.

"Get the pistols," Mr. Corduroy said. "Vera, GET THE PISTOLS!"

The blue-haired lady nodded and then slowly – very slowly – rose from her chair. Then she slowly – verrrrrry slowly – walked over to a chest in the corner that was meant to be used by visiting great-grandchildren. Then, verrrrrrrrrrrrrrrry slowly, she dug to the bottom and pulled out a pair of water pistols.

Then she went to the kitchenette and filled them with tomato juice.

"Stains more," she explained.

We were handed the pistols. Wheelchair guy guarded the door.

"Ten paces," the cougher told us.

Solemnly, we placed ourselves back-to-back.

The blue-haired lady began to count.

One. Two. Three. Four. Five.

We stepped farther and farther apart.

Six. Seven. Eight.

I was doing this for Lily.

Nine.

I was not going to waste my shot.

Ten.

I pivoted. Got him in my sights. Pulled the trigger at the same time he pulled his.

We both . . . trickled.

Someone had forgotten to give our pistols their Viagra.

"ARRRRRRR!" Thibaud yelled, storming toward me.

"Ahhhhhhh!" I yelled, running away.

I pushed past Wheelchair Guy, into the hallway.

Smirking Sadie was out a-strolling, and she let out a yelp when she saw me plunging pistol-forward. I wanted Thibaud to shoot while we were on the run, to vac8 all his V8. But he was saving it for closer range.

I was not going to be his quarry.

"In the name of all that's good and Lily!" I proclaimed, copping my best Young Han Solo pose and blasting away.

This time the trigger cocked, and the TJ flew forth.

Unfortunately, by proclaiming my attack, I'd given Thibaud time to dodge.

"Not so fast, milquetoast!" he growled. I feinted left, rocked right. He missed.

At this point, an orderly named Caleb saw the Bloody Mary flying through the air and screamed bloody murder at us. Thibaud went for another shot. I blocked it with an errant cafeteria tray. But this blocked my own shot, so I had to drop it.

Thibaud raised his pistol again. Ran forward. And slipped on the puddles we'd made.

From somewhere in the darkest depths of my soul, I unearthed the phrase, "Sugar, you're going down!"

Thibaud screamed. Caleb the orderly screamed. Smirking Sadie called out, "Vera, you really gotta see this!"

I aimed. He writhed. I fired.

Eye of the bull.

As he was drenched, I slipped and I slid. He grabbed at my legs. I wobbled and fell.

I made sure to land on him.

"Seriously, though," I said once our breath returned from being knocked out, "I've vanquished you."

"Okay, you got me," Thibaud conceded. "What do I have to do?"

"You," I grunted, "have to throw us a party."

Thursday, December 18th

"You're not seeing what's in front of you," I told her. "First of all, this *is* a Christmas sweater. Just because it's not showy – just because it doesn't have tinsel or lights or a big bad reindeer on it – that doesn't mean it's not a Christmas sweater. The truth doesn't have to advertise itself. All the truth needs to be is true."

Lily looked so lost. "What are you doing? Why are you doing this?"

Finally I was able to tell her what I'd been going to tell her all along.

"Lily," I said, "this is an intervention."

"An intervention?" Lily asked, thoroughly confused.

"A Divine intervention!" Boomer cried. "But not in the *Pink Flamingos* sense!"

"What Boomer means," I said, "is that we're all here for you. Well, I think a few of Thibaud's friends came for the beer. But the rest of us wanted to show you a good time. No – scratch that. We didn't want to show you a good

118

time – we wanted you to *feel* a good time. And I thought you were having a good time, which – and correct me if I'm wrong here – doesn't feel like the right lead-in for breaking up with me."

I looked at Sofia for confirmation that I was doing this right. She gave me a little nod.

Lily turned to Thibaud. "*You* were in on this?"

Thibaud tried to brush it off. "You could say I was pistol-whipped into doing it. But whatever. As I read once in a bathroom stall, *For a good time, call Edgar.* How could your quote-boyfriend-unquote resist?"

"If you don't take those quotes out, next time we'll duel with rapiers!" I threatened, perhaps a little overconfident of my rapier talents.

"You dueled?" Lily asked.

"Yes. And if we do it again, it will be –"

"DON'T SAY IT!" Thibaud screamed.

"– a dual duel," I completed, with satisfaction.

"Dash!" Boomer cried. "Not the point!"

I turned to Lily. "Yes. That's not the point. The point is that I really don't want you to break up with me. In fact, what I'd like is for us to do the opposite of break up with each other."

"Break into each other!" Boomer offered.

Both Lily and I shivered in horror at this wording. I figured that was a good sign.

*

Friday, December 19th

We met in the park to wrest the afternoon into the shape of a stroll. I'd had to go to school. She'd had to sneak out from being grounded.

We walked down to the duck pond at the bottom of the park. Remembering the author who'd brought us together (in some way), I was going to remark to her that I always wondered where the ducks went when winter came. Because there weren't supposed to be any ducks, not at this time of year.

But this time, there was a swan. A single swan.

Thursday, December 18th

I looked at my watch. "Curfew's coming," I pointed out. Then I smiled. "But there's always time for one more dance, right?"

Leave it to Thibaud to cue up the season's stupidest new song, an R&B jam called "Santa Can't Feel His Face."

Too much snow, girl
And Santa can't feel his face
Wind's full of blow, girl
And Santa can't feel his face

Thibaud grinned – one should never leave the details to the devil. But I wasn't going to be deterred. I wrapped my arms around Lily – and her sweater was so tight that I felt I was touching her, no protective layer. Body music finding its groove.

"This song is the worst!" Lily said.

"There's no one I'd rather share it with than you!" I swore.

Snow down the chimney
White Christmas of your dreams
And Santa can't feel his face
But he's still on the ride

Friday, December 19th

"Do you see that?" I said. But of course Lily saw the swan. Carefully, we approached. It was now cold enough for us to wear gloves. Now I took her gloved hand in mine.

"What is it doing here?" she asked.

"A little lost?" I offered. "Or maybe it just wanted to see the Bergdorf windows like everyone else on Fifth Avenue."

The swan saw us. It glided across the surface of the unfrozen pond, beholding us with a cold curiosity.

Lily disengaged her hand so she could take a picture.

But before she could, it began to sing.

Thursday, December 18th

The song ended. I still held on. At least for an extra moment. Then it was awkward, since Thibaud was stranding us without a new song.

"I take it back," Lily said.

But the thing was: She didn't sound certain.

I let her take it back anyway.

121

The only problem with taking something back?

It's still inside there somewhere.

Friday, December 19th

The swan began to sing, and it wasn't a honk or a squawk or a dirge. It had a tune. It was something between a lament and a hosanna.

When it was done, I applauded. Because I was wearing gloves, it didn't make much of a sound.

Lily looked concerned.

"What's wrong?" I asked.

"It's going to die. It sings a beautiful song . . . and then it dies."

"That's just a phrase," I assured her.

The swan went back to ignoring us. It went back to swimming. It stayed afloat.

Saturday, December 20th

The next morning, Lily went missing again.

8
LILY

Lilymaid a-Milking

Saturday, December 20th

You're missing again, said the text from my brother.

I didn't answer.

I'm staying at Benny's tonight. We're planning our new apartment and I'm not going out searching for you.

I still didn't answer.

I see the dot dot dot. I know you see this message.

Stalker Brother, a new movie-by-text, streaming now on iMessage.

This is getting annoying, Lily Bear. You're crossing that fine line from adorable to obnoxious.

Said by every adult to every teenager, ever.

My brother was ready to move into his own apartment. He was one of them now.

I rolled my eyes and turned off my phone.

I wasn't missing.

I was lost.

*

Five days before Christmas, and excitement should have been building, but all I felt was doom and gloom. I'd yet to bake my favorite lebkuchen cookies, wander the holiday stalls in Union Square, go ice-skating in Central Park – numbers two, six, and eight in my top ten favorite holiday traditions that herald the arrival of the Great Present Exchange (number one, obviously) of December 25. I hadn't even made a wish list of what I wanted. I hadn't joined my caroling society for singing excursions – and I was the founding member of the group.

I had been intervened about my Christmas blues, making me only bluer.

My Grandpa had decamped for his sister's house with his cat, and I had let him, without running after him to beg him to stay with us, or begging for his forgiveness for worrying him when I disappeared to Staten Island, or at least insisting he leave the cat with me.

I didn't know who I was anymore.

Dash knows how I hate seeing animals suffer, and yet I didn't tell him how upsetting I thought our visit with the swan in the park had been. Like, I wanted to be sick about it afterward, but I said nothing to Dash at the end of our walk besides, "See ya later, I guess." We just were not connecting, and I couldn't fake it any longer. I had to get away.

"You're getting *everything wrong.*" Dash's words repeated in my head like the earworm of that mean guy calling *Alviiiiiin* the chipmunk to attention.

"You're getting *everything wrong.*"

Alviiiiin!

"You're getting *everything wrong.*"

Alviiiiin!

Please, Lily's brain. BE QUIET.

I was almost irritated enough to turn my phone back on to correct Langston, to remind him I have a dog, and dogs I walk, and I would never willfully go missing on them. I might ignore the people in my life, but I would never disregard my responsibilities to my fur babies. Boris had not only been walked early this morning. I'd taken him for a long run and play at the off-leash dog park all the way over on Randall's Island, which required two very expensive taxi rides because the New York City Transit Authority says pets are only allowed on public transportation if they are "enclosed in a container and carried in a manner which would not annoy other passengers." The first part Boris could handle; the second part he could not. So now there are two very not-happy taxi drivers because of large Boris's small farting and slobbering problem, and the exchange of smelly and wet dollar bills from my purse, which Boris had been sitting on during the rides. But Boris was so tired out from the excursion, he would be sleeping for the rest of the day and not even notice I was gone, so why was my brother worried if I wasn't home and didn't tell him where I'd gone?

And seriously, if my family just checked with my dog-walking clients, who received dutiful texts this morning letting them know I was not available today, along with a list of alternate, responsible dog walkers, they'd know I was not missing. Missing implies unintentional gone-away-ness. Like when a girl mistakenly ingests hallucinogenic gingerbread men and then her intentional day away turns into legit overnight missing.

Maybe that's my real problem. Not that I'm lost but that possibly now I'm an addict, craving more and more wild experiences. Danger. Risk. More Jahna, less Lily.

I sighed, and could see my breath in the cold air of the train car. Freezing winter had finally arrived, but the mean kind. Bitter, single-digit temps that kept the train moving slowly because of signal problems, and kept the few people on the barely heated train huddling under their down coats, tying their scarves tightly across their heads and necks and rubbing their gloved hands together. Nobody talked; they just teeth-chattered and shivered.

The air felt as cold as my heart. I looked out the window at the afternoon sun, beaming brightly, as if to say, *Here I am, your master of light, so big and powerful that I can radiate no warmth whatsoever if I so choose, and just to be spiteful, I'm going to block any possibility of snow to go along with this frigid cold. Who owns winter? I own winter, that's who. Suck it, humans of the northeast Atlantic!*

I wanted to cry, but was afraid the tears would freeze on my face. Dash was right. I *was* getting everything wrong. I couldn't read him at all, and I couldn't even break up with him convincingly, because I was a neurotic mess who loved him too much to insist he let me go, for both our sakes.

The train pulled into its next stop. At first I thought

I had imagined it, so I took my glasses off and cleaned them with a tissue and put them back on. Indeed, the sign on the Metro North platform said PLEASANTVILLE. That was really a place? And if so, why were an army of noisy, angry, drunken Santas getting on? I mean, every kind of Santa – male, female, young, old, fat, skinny, from fully-dressed Santas with long white beards to practically naked, almost-a-stripper Santas. More disturbingly, the Santas were followed by a group of carousing carolers tossing hooch flasks to each other as they sang a ditty I know for a fact was not true to the era of the singers' Victorian costumes.

The kids cry
The reindeers lie
Only the missus knows why
And Santa can't feel his face

Enough with that song already. It's worse than *Alviiiiin*. So disrespectful. And catchy!

The train conductor entered behind the crowd surge and announced, "Next stop, Chappaqua!" When none of the embarking passengers budged, he said, louder, "Anyone who *thinks* they're on the train to Manhattan should know that train is *on the other platform*." Still, no one exited. The train conductor tried one more time. "This is *not* the Manhattan train. Unless you're going upstate, you oughta get off now. Last call, Wassaic." The Santas and carolers settled into seats. "Damn," the train conductor said, and left the car.

A late-middle-aged male caroler dressed in a Victorian-era suit and top hat sat down next to me. He tipped his top hat to me. "Merry Christmas, darlin'. I'm Wassail from Wassaic." His breath smelled like Jack Daniel's from Tennessee (and not the fancy Sinatra Century Limited Edition variety).

I wasn't sure if he was teasing about his name, and it's hard to get a straight answer from straight-up drunks. So while the train conductor had made it pretty clear, I tried also. I wasn't so lost that I wasn't fully aware what today was. Trying to be helpful, I told Wassail from Wassaic, "If you're going to SantaCon, you need to be on the train going to Manhattan. On the other platform."

My seatmate scoffed. "We *were* on the train to Grand Central, a coupla hours ago. We got kicked off in Mount Kisco."

"But this is Pleasantville."

"Isn't it? We barhopped our way down here, and then decided to try again going to the city. But a little fight erupted between the Santas and the carolers – lots of gang warfare this year, sorry to say. And the grand marshal in charge of the Wassaic brigade decided it was better to abandon our mission altogether."

"Better to end up passed out on Metro North than wake up in jail in the city?" I asked him.

"Ah, yer a pretty and smart sassy lassie," he said, looking and sounding more like a lecherous Irish leprechaun than a chivalrous Victorian English gentleman.

A goth lady Santa with a pierced lip, tunneled ears, and black spiked hair popped her head up from the seat in front of us. She pointed at my seatmate. "Don't be a wasshole, Wassail," she said. "Don't hit on a child!"

"I'm doing no such thing!" Wassail said, indignant.

"You are!" said a platoon of Santas in our perimeter.

"I'm not a child," I mumbled.

I didn't want the gang warfare to spiral out of control, so at long last, the childish Lily from the days of yore emerged from her holiday-resistance stupor. If there was one thing she knew how to do, it was carol her way out of trouble.

I sang, *Here we come a-wassailing / Among the leaves so green!*

Goth-Santa shot devil eyes at me, but the Victorian carolers immediately picked up the song. *Here we come a-wand'ring / So fair to be seen.*

I mean, it was impossible not to feel the mood change, from drunk and cold and restless, to drunk and cold and verging on festive.

At least half the train car – including many Santas – joined in. *Love and joy come to you / And to you your wassail, too, / And God bless you, and send you / A Happy New Year.*

Wassail from Wassaic stood up and bowed at the end of the verse, like it had been written just for him.

No one continued singing after the second verse. Old Lily – aka Third-Verse Lily – might have continued on anyway, but was silenced by a Victorian gown-wearing lady whose bonnet had just been yanked off her head, who

129

delivered a sudden, epic slap to the red face of a portly Santa wearing angel wings on his back.

"Can Santa feel his face now?" Vicky shrieked at fat Santa angel.

"Fight! Fight!" the drunks chanted.

I'm all for drunk people, but the jolly kind, not the contentious kind.

I really wanted my mommy.

I emerged from the train at the end of the line in Wassaic. Wassail from Wassaic and his not-merry band of SantaCon artists and raucous carolers did not follow me off the train. They'd been kicked out at Katonah.

My mother was waiting in the parking lot, shivering inside her rental car. "Your train was an hour late."

"The bitter cold weather is causing delays," I said. "And some drunken Santas that had to be kicked off the train."

"Was SantaCon today?" Mom said. I nodded. "Good day to be gone from the city. Like the streets aren't packed enough at this time of the year. They were cute at first. Now they're nuisances."

I saw the ends of a cocktail dress peeking from beneath Mom's long, heavy coat, and she wore fancy high-heeled shoes on her feet. I knew Mom had more important places she was supposed to be, but I was having an existential crisis. I needed her more. "Thanks for meeting me at such short notice. You didn't say anything to Dad or Langston, right?"

Mom shook her head. She couldn't outright say no to my

question, because we'd both know she was lying, like when she swore to me she hadn't told them when I got my first bra and my first period, but she totally had. Mom said, "I've got an hour, tops. Dad's entertaining financial donors now, so I don't need to be there for that, but I have to get back in time for the start of the faculty party, if I still want to be married by the end of it. So unless you want to come with me and be paraded around as the headmaster's daughter, I'm going to have to put you back on the train to Manhattan in an hour."

"I understand." Along with all my other faults of late, I was wasting my mother's lovely party dress and face on sitting in a car with sullen me. "You look very pretty." My mother usually goes for the yoga-pants-and-loose-shirts-with-unbrushed-hair-pulled-back-in-a-bun look, but when she puts on some mascara and lipstick and blows out her hair, it's like, Wow, Mom, you're a babe!

"Thank you. I got you this." Mom handed me a paper coffee cup that had a molasses cookie on top of it.

"It's coffee? This cup is cold." She was being so nice to me when I didn't deserve it, so I don't know why I was acting so whiny besides that I was having an existential crisis *and* I'm just moody and awful.

"It's supposed to be. Before your train pulled in, there was a hipster coffee truck parked across the street. They were making holiday-themed drinks for the passengers headed into the city. I got their last two gingerbread lattes before they closed up."

"Where's yours?"

"It was so good I finished it in about one minute flat. Say what you will about hipsters, but those suspender-wearing beardies really know how to pull an artisanal brew."

"It looks weird for a latte," I said, suspiciously eyeing the creamy dollop in the cup.

"Stop pouting and just try it. 'Latte' is a misnomer. It's actually an ice-cream shake made with espresso mixed with some kind of vanilla ice cream, with bits of malted milk balls and candied ginger pieces mixed in."

Sold! I dunked the cookie into the drink and then took a bite. "Oh my God! This is possibly the best drink I've ever had in my life." I silently included in that calculation the one time I got drunk last year on peppermint schnapps, which tasted like a peppermint patty in a beverage. Heaven. This gingerbread latte was heaven-squared. "You're the best, Mom."

"Is that a smile I see on your face? It's been a long time since I've seen it, so I'm not sure."

I gulped down the remainder of the latte, not caring if the rush of the consumption would give me an ice-cream headache. I licked my lips. "Smiling!" I said. Add to my list of mental woes: My moods could swing violently from sulking to delirious with the right infusion of sugar.

Teenage hormones. I don't know. They're exhausting trying to monitor.

Mom said, "If I'd known all it took was a gingerbread latte, I'd have hunted down that coffee truck a long time ago." She worriedly looked at the time on the car dashboard, and then her face turned serious. "So what's going on, Lily? You've got my full attention until the 2:37. I'm worried about you."

"I'm worried about me, too."

She placed her hands over the car heater, and then pressed her warmed hands on my cold cheeks. They felt so good. "Tell me, sweetheart. Is this about Langston moving? Or Dad and me possibly moving up here? Or Grandpa? You understand that heart attack victims often get depressed and angry as they recover? He's not himself anymore."

"I'm upset about all that. But no."

"So we're not the center of your life anymore?" she asked gently.

"Not exactly," I admitted.

"Ah," said Mom. "Dashiell."

Moms always know.

"I tried to break up with him. He said no!"

"Really? That's a surprise." I wasn't sure if she was surprised I'd want to break up with him or that he'd refused me. "What did you say to him?"

"I said, 'I think we should break up.'"

"Doesn't sound like a convincing breakup directive to me. What did Dash say to that?"

"He said no, and that I was getting everything wrong. But he didn't say what exactly."

"I don't understand. Why'd you want to break up with him in the first place? I know the men in our family try not to like him despite themselves, but *I* think he seems lovely.

And pretty devoted to you."

"That's the problem!" I felt the cold, bitter tears forming in my eyes, and I didn't care if they froze my face. They needed to come out. "Dash likes. I . . . *love.*"

"Oh, honey." Mom wiped the tears from my face and pulled me to her for a hug. "Did you tell him that?"

"I tried. Once. It was like he didn't hear me. And he never said it back. And it hurts so much to love someone who doesn't love you back, Mom!" It was such a relief to just say it out loud. Already I felt better, despite how bruised my heart was.

"Honey, I know you're hurting, but think about it. Is saying 'I love you' really what defines a relationship? It's the actions, not the words."

"But Dash is a man of words!"

Mom's face reflected the bitter truth of my comment. "That's true," she admitted. "But how do you know he doesn't feel the same way about you? Maybe he thinks you already know. It seems obvious to everyone else."

I knew she was just saying that to make me feel better. It was nice. I appreciated her comfort, even though it was misguided. "I can't talk to him about it!"

"But why not? He's your boyfriend. I don't understand."

It took a moment to finally admit the real truth. "Because then he'll just see what a clingy, insecure mess I am."

"I'd hardly call you that."

"That's what I feel like! I used to feel sorry for girls who went all stupid when they got boyfriends. Now I've become one of those girls! One who needs him to tell her he loves her because she's so neurotic she has to hear it from him to feel, like, validated in her feelings for him. I *hate* that!" I didn't know what was wrong with me. I'd never confided in my mom like this before. Those drunk Santas must have infected me with their lack of restraint. Mom laughed. "There's nothing funny about this," I reminded her.

"I know," she said, down-turning her lips to a neutral, serious position. "It's just that you're reminding me of when I was first going out with your dad, and starting to have deep feelings for him. We'd been dating for a few months, and then out of nowhere, I turned brutally cold and broke up with him. I didn't want to let him in that close."

"And your family is a lot of baggage to bring to somebody," I said. My other fear with Dash: My family. *His* family.

"There's that," Mom allowed. "It took a while before I invited him to Christmas, and to meet aunts and uncles and cousin after cousin. He still hasn't recovered from the shock of the sheer numbers of us."

"Dash's family is toxic."

"That doesn't mean he is."

"I know. But it's unsettling to see how mean his parents are to each other. What if he turns out like his dad?"

"As much as I haven't been ready for you to have a boyfriend, I'm giving this one to Dash. He's *nothing* like his dad. Except for the color of his eyes."

"But Dash's eyes are so beautiful!" I was ready to

sob again.

"What do you really want from me, Lily? For me to talk you into or out of this relationship?"

"I want Dash to know what to say and what to do! I want him to know to take me to see *Corgi & Bess* and make it special. I want him to not just bring me a Christmas tree, but stay awhile and stop time to be just with me." It was like I wasn't even talking to Mom anymore. I ranted, "Don't just show me you adore me. Tell me you love me, or break up with me and put me out of this misery of wanting to give my whole heart to you and you just being like, 'Oh, what a cute Lily heart you are so naïvely holding out to me. You don't mind if I throw it on the ground and stomp all over it, do you?'"

Mom paused, and I think she was trying to suppress a laugh, but she at least made a face like she was waiting so she could formulate a thoughtful response. Finally she said, "First of all, it's not fair to expect Dash to be psychic about what you really want from him. Second, and this is just a broader piece of advice for you about anyone you might date, but any male who automatically knows how to tick off all the items on your female wish-fulfillment list is too good to be true. It's not natural to their species, and you should find it highly suspicious if he does. Third, if you feel so strongly about him, I think it's *your* responsibility to be honest with him about it and not wait for him to tell you something he has no idea you're waiting to hear."

"But what if Dash doesn't feel the same way?"

"That's a risk you have to take. This is one of those moments when you get to decide who you want to be. It's like an awkward, uncomfortable growth spurt, but one that ultimately moves you in a definitive direction. Are you going to be someone who takes charge of her feelings and her actions, even if the outcome might hurt, or someone who lets herself be unhappy simply because she won't ask for what she wants?"

"They both sound like sucky options."

Mom no longer looked like she was trying not to laugh. She said, very seriously, "I see now the danger in letting you be so overprotected. It taught you to overprotect your heart."

"I'm scared."

"You should be. There's nothing more frightening than true intimacy."

"MOM!" I couldn't be more embarrassed. "That's not what I meant!"

"That's not what I meant either. I'm talking about emotional intimacy, not physical. Acknowledging how you really feel, who you really are. Opening up your soul to another person. There's nothing scarier. And I've been to Woodbury Common outlet mall on Black Friday. I know from scary."

I had nothing to say while I absorbed what she'd said. To my silence, Mom added, "But since *you* brought it up – "

"No, we haven't!" I said, squirming. "I mean, he doesn't even, like, protest about your rule that my bedroom door has to be open if we're in there alone together."

"That's your dad's rule, not mine, but I can't say I blame Dash. I don't think I'd want to fool around with you in your bedroom either if I knew you had a dozen family members outside the door waiting to strangle him if he tried anything beyond holding your hand."

I honestly wanted to convulse with grossness hearing my mother say the words "fool around" in the context of Dash and me, but I also liked the other part of what she was suggesting. "So Dash can be in my bedroom with the door closed?"

"If he dares. Sure. I overrule Dad on this one. Dash is a good guy, and if you're ready to have this conversation about intimacy with me, then I trust you to make the best decision when the time is right for both of you, and to handle it responsibly. But I'm guessing there're other places Dash would rather be alone with you. I wouldn't take his indifference to the open door to mean his lack of desire for you."

Our hour was up. We could hear the 2:37 Manhattan-bound train approaching in the far-off distance.

"Are you really moving up here?" I asked Mom.

"Still haven't decided. But I admit I like it more than I expected. It's hard commuting across Long Island just to be an untenured community college instructor teaching undergrads who need English credits, but could care less about the great sonnets. I might like to be an unemployed poet up here instead."

"But your family is in the city."

"Dad wants to be here. That's the risk I have to take. Choose him. Old people like us have these hard growth spurts, too."

"But Grandpa!"

Mom sighed. "He's gotten so obstinate. We all know the best place for him would be an assisted-living facility. Better quality of life for him."

I gasped. "He'd be so mad if he heard you say that!"

"I know. That's a big part of the problem. Not seeing that what's best for him is what also would be better for everybody. He's needing more care than we can reliably give him, despite how much we love him. We all stopped our lives after his fall, but at some point we have to choose to lead our own lives again, as painful as that choice will be."

"Where will I go?"

"You can move up here and go to Dad's school. Or you could live at Mrs. Basil E.'s and spend the summer with us. She's offered. You're a big girl now. You can figure it out. No one's abandoning you, and everyone will do everything possible to make the situation work for you. Because that's how awesome your family is, and why you should never ever again go missing from them."

There was too much still to discuss, and about one minute left before I had to get out of the car to catch the train. So I focused on the important issue.

"Am I still grounded?"

"Yes."

"Really?" I made a sad, Lily's-falling-into-an-emotional-tailspin-again face.

"No. And don't think I'm not aware of what you're doing."

"What's that?"

"Lilymaid's a-milking Mom's sympathies for all she can. Now go home and get your Christmas on, finally. And tell Dash –"

I kissed her cheek. "Bye, Mom. Thank you. I love you."

I dashed out of the car toward the train, to dash me home to Dash.

Once I got on the train, I turned on my phone again. My heart was ready to explode for everything I wanted to tell Dash. I was ungrounded, I had the apartment to myself, and I loved a boy.

The first text message I saw was from Dash. My heart leapt just at the sight of his name, and I thought of how brave I was going to be when I saw him next. Then my heart sank when I read his words. *I try so hard to make you happy. But clearly I can't. I don't want to say you're impossible to please. But you're impossible to please. And since you can't stop disappearing, I realized you're right. We need a break.*

9
DASH

It Takes Two to Tangle

Saturday, December 20th

I paused my texting, then continued.

That break will last exactly twenty-three hours. No longer. No less.

"Did I get the math right?" I asked Mrs. Basil E., showing her the phone.

"Yes. Now . . . the final touch."

"But of course!"

Further instructions to follow, I typed.

SEND.

I waited to see if Lily would respond.

She did not.

"I really hope this works," I said.

Mrs. Basil E. looked up at me from her settee, and it was clear she did not want me to be a regrettee.

"You must give it your all. But please note where I put emphasis in that sentence. For your benefit, I shall repeat: You must give it *your* all."

"But didn't we just establish that she's impossible to please?"

"People who want things to be perfect are always impossible to please. But that doesn't mean we should stop trying. Even if their expectations aren't correct, their instincts are. You won't get everything right, Dash. Even Lily knows that. The trying is what matters."

"It's the thought that counts, then."

"Ah, but have you ever tried counting thoughts? They are extraordinarily hard to wrangle."

I would have sat back and sighed, but I was perched on a glorified footstool, so sitting back was not an option, and sighing only would have been labeled a melodramatic self-indulgence by my interlocutor.

Instead I said, "I just feel like this is my last chance." Which, once it was out of my mouth, also sounded like melodramatic self-indulgence . . . but also happened to be a bona fide truth.

"Here's the thing about love," Mrs. Basil E. replied. "You get a last chance. And then, when that doesn't work, you make yourself another last chance. Then another. Then another. You keep going until your last chances run out."

"But if there are many of them, doesn't that mean that only the last one is actually –"

"I am not trying to make a grammatical point here," Mrs. Basil E. hushed. "I am trying to make an *emotional* point. I don't expect you to understand me on that level – you are but a romantic sapling. I am a sequoia, so you'd be well advised to listen to what I have to say."

"Your experience runs rings around mine."

"Precisely."

I stood up from my ottomanopoeic perch. "I appreciate your help."

Mrs. Basil E. stood as well. "And I appreciate your appreciation. Now, let us get to work. We have a lot of logistics to contend with. Twenty-three hours seems like a long time, but it's nothing, Dash. It's the time it takes a book to fall off a shelf."

I looked at my phone. Still no response.

Mrs. Basil E. put her hand on my arm. A light but definitive touch.

"She'll come," she assured me. "She doesn't realize either that this isn't a last, last chance. She's also a sapling. But that's the beauty of your young love – you can learn to be trees together."

"If this works."

"Yes, if this works."

Sunday, December 21st

I met Langston in front of the Strand. Not only is the Strand the site of the start of my and Lily's origin story, but it also happens to be the best bookstore in the world, a wonderland for the literate and the literary. If this was going to be a last chance, I wanted to go back to the first chance, and to have all the possibility of that first chance come alive a year later.

Langston held a box in his hand. Lifting it to show me, he said, "Are you sure this is necessary?"

I knew this was hard for him. I knew the contents of the box were deeply precious to him.

"Mark has promised he'll watch over it," I told him. "The only hands it will fall into are Lily's."

"But why does it have to be Joey? He was a vintage boy-band relic when my friend Elizabeth gave him to me back in fifth grade. Now he's, like, *super* vintage."

"The whole point is that Lily will know it's yours. She'll know we're all in this together."

Langston knew this, but it was still hard for him. He didn't hand over the prize until we were up in the YA section, with his cousin Mark glowering at our side.

"I have no idea why I'm helping you," Mark coughed up. "But here I am, helping you. It's an affront to every strain of my insouciance."

Still, even Mark was reverent when Langston pulled the Joey McIntyre doll from its packaging.

"Take care," Langston whispered in Joey's ear. "Remember, this is for Lily."

I took a copy of *Baby Be-Bop* out of my bag, removed the dust jacket, then wrapped the dust jacket around a red Moleskine notebook. From there, we put everything in place.

"You are not to let Joey out of your sight," Langston instructed Mark.

"You're treating him like he's Timberlake," Mark grumbled. "But fine."

"And you're to send word the minute she shows," I reminded him.

"*If* she shows," Mark corrected, enjoying his italics.

"If," I agreed.

I couldn't stop to worry about it. There were too many other things to do, in too short a time.

Twenty-two hours and fifty-seven minutes after my previous text, I sent Lily a new one:

Forget the elf on the shelf.

Go to where it all began and look for a New Kid on the Block.

I didn't have time to wait for a reply. I'd pushed over the first domino – now I had to hope that the others would be in the right place to fall.

My next stop was Boomer. He was, perhaps, the riskiest domino of all, as far as a tendency to walk off the path.

The ranks of Oscar's comrades had thinned considerably, so the streetside forest Boomer had manned a few days ago was now a sub-arbor. Still, his spirit remained undiminished.

"I still have three days to find them all homes!" Boomer whispered to me, as if he were operating a log shelter.

I took a square Tupperware container out of my bag and opened it to show Boomer its contents.

"Oh!" he exclaimed. "Scented woodchips."

I stared at him for a second.

"Are they not woodchips? Are they petrified reindeer doo?"

I gulped.

"It's funny, because they look like they're in the shape of letters!"

"Yes," I said. "They *are* in the shape of letters. They're a clue."

"But why would you spell a clue out in reindeer poo?"

"It's not *reindeer poo*! I made cookies."

Now Boomer started to crack up. Not a snide snicker. Not an amateur tee-hee-hee. No, Boomer started laughing from his diaphragm, then threw his whole body into it.

"Cookies!" he said when he had enough breath to talk. "Those are . . . the ugliest cookies . . . I've ever seen!"

"They're lebkuchen!" I cried out. "Or at least they're lebkuchenesque! It's a recipe from Nuremberg! I mean, Nuremberg by way of the Martha Stewart website! According to Martha's minions, they date back to the fourteenth century!"

Boomer calmed down and took another look inside the Tupperware, this time as if it were a reliquary. "Oh . . . that explains it," he said solemnly. "They're from the fourteenth century!"

"Not these specific cookies!" I looked at them again – and had to concede (to myself, not to Boomer) that they had a Gothic air about them. In my haste to make them the previous night, I'd had to substitute some ingredients (because, unlike Martha, I didn't happen to have four medjool dates sitting around in my kitchen), and I could see how the results looked

like a bread lover's idea of what gluten-free is.

"I can't let her eat those," Boomer said. "She might get sick. Or angry."

"They're not to eat. They're to *read*." I arranged them in order on the bottom of the Tupperware.

"'WAM MA'AM THANK YOU BAM!'" Boomer read. Then he added, "Shouldn't the 'wam' have an *h*, like 'where' or 'what' or 'wherewolf'?"

"I burned the *h* beyond recognition, okay? Meanwhile, do you remember your line?"

"'Lily, do you need some clarification?'"

"No – 'clar*a*fication.'"

"'Clarification.'"

"'Clar-A-fication.'"

"'Clar-*A*-fication.'"

"Perfect. And if she says yes?"

"I say, 'I'd like to crack that one in the nuts!'"

"No. 'That's a hard nut to crack!'"

"'You crack me up with your nuts!'"

"'*That's a hard nut to crack*.'"

"'Your nuts are so hard right now!'"

"Boomer. You are *not* to say 'Your nuts are so hard right now!' to Lily. Do you understand?"

"Maybe you should write it down and I can just hand it over?"

"Good idea."

As I was writing it down on the back of a receipt from Blick, my phone buzzed.

The Boy Band is Dead, Mark wrote. *Long Live the Boy Band.*

What do u mean? I typed back.

That's Bieber, not Boy Band, Mark replied.

Enough pop semantics, Langston interrupted, since this was a group message. *Is Joey on the move?*

He's hanging tough with our girl, Mark answered. *And they've got a red Moleskine to read.*

I was amazed at how relieved I felt. Something was happening. Lily and I needed something to happen, and now something was happening.

"Okay, Boomer, I gotta go," I said.

"Aw, jeez, Dash, I'm sorry – we don't have a bathroom."

"Not *that* kind of 'gotta go.' This is more the 'I have to be somewhere else' kind."

"Well, I hope they have a bathroom there!"

"They do," I assured him. "They have a few."

I knew there was no way for me to follow Lily's path, not if I wanted to end up where I needed to be.

There were three clues between the Strand and Boomer, and Lily picked them off one by one.

Go to the 92 to see the 10th and 11th candles.

(Our unorthodox Orthodox Jewish friends Dov and Yohnny were next to the big menorah in the lobby of the 92nd Street Y, holding up candles and a clue.)

It's time for the other boot to fall . . . in the same place you lost the first one.

(Sofia had sweet-talked the owner of a popular club to let Lily in during the day. Mrs. Basil E. had loaned me a boot of hers to place in the restroom stall where I'd left a message for Lily a year ago. That message had said *Please return the notebook to the handsome gumshoe wearing the fedora hat.* Now Sofia had traced my handwriting to write, *The Little Foxes want you to know this isn't a dead end. The children's hour may be over, but there's still time for frozen hot chocolate.*)

(That would lead to Serendipity – because everyone in New York knows there's only one place in Manhattan to get frozen hot chocolate. There, Lily's grandfather would be waiting at a table – Sofia would text him to get the frozen hot chocolate ready. He was instructed not to talk about the red notebook with Lily, but to talk about anything else she wanted to talk about. Then, when the bill came, the waiter would have written the next clue on the back of the receipt – *If a tree falls in the forest, who's most likely to go over to it to see if it's okay?*)

That would lead to Boomer.

And Boomer would lead to Brooklyn.

Boomer texted me as I got off the subway.

The good news is she's on her way. She didn't even ask for clarAfication.

I waited for the bad news.

And waited.

Finally I typed, *What's the bad news?*

Oh yeah! The bad news is that even though I warned her hard against it, she tried one of the cookies.

I didn't have time to worry about this – baking prowess had never been the basis of our relationship, so I hadn't really compromised much by showing her the limits of my flouring. Instead I headed over to the Brooklyn Academy of Music – BAM, for short – and prepared for Lily's arrival.

The current production at BAM was the Mark Morris Dance Group's production of *The Nutcracker,* called *The Hard Nut*. It took the familiar *Nutcracker* story and moved it to a wacky suburban house in the 1970s. One of the big scenes was a swingin' holiday party that went tipsily awry. Another involved Marie, the Clara of this *Nutcracker*, holding her own against the Rat King with only a flashlight to defend herself.

The stage looked like a cartoon version of a 1970s sitcom home – everything a little larger than life. But there was a tree, and under the tree were presents.

One of them was for Lily.

This was the most elaborate part of the plan. Luckily, Mrs. Basil E. had an in with BAM. ("I've supported the arts for so long, it's only natural that I should call on the arts to support me," she explained.) Lauren, the dancer who played Marie, let me into the theater. When Lily arrived, she would find David, the dancer who was the Nutcracker Prince, waiting to guide her to the stage. Then he'd disappear, and everyone else would wait in the wings. This was a run-through that wasn't usually open to the public, and they were adding an extra character for a short time.

I took my place in the highest balcony of the otherwise empty opera house. Langston, Sofia, Boomer, Mrs. Basil E., Dov, and Yohnny were all texting me from afar to see how it was going. I gave them a quick update, then turned off my phone.

I almost didn't hear the door opening. From my perch, I couldn't see Lily at first – only when she walked down the aisle toward the stage. She held the red Moleskine in one hand, Joey McIntyre in the other. From so far away, it was hard to read her expression.

There was a single spotlight haloing the tree. Lily walked the stairs to the stage, then looked around to see if anyone else was there. The spotlight narrowed to focus on a single present, and Lily stepped toward it. If you squinted, you could imagine she was Clara, woken on Christmas morning. When you opened your eyes, you could see that she was grown up, nearly an adult. But with the same wonder showing in her movements, because that's not something you have to grow out of.

I had wrapped the box with the recipe for lebkuchen cookies. Inside was another box, wrapped in quotations from *Baby Be-Bop*. Then another box, with wrapping paper I'd saved from FAO Schwarz. And an even smaller box, wrapped in a newspaper advertisement for *Corgi & Bess*. Finally, the smallest box of all, with her name on its lid in my handwriting.

She opened it. Took out the envelope. Opened the card

and read the two words I'd written before signing my name. A gift card fell out of it. She took a look, saw where it was from and what the amount was.

Smiled.

Then, as if knowing I would want to be there to see her smile, she looked up. I thought for sure I'd be caught, and wasn't sure whether or not that was a bad thing. But as her eyes lifted into the eaves, the lights on the stage burst alive and Tchaikovsky began to play. Startled, Lily pulled back to the tree.

The snowdrop fairies began to dance.

This was my favorite part of the ballet. I knew it would be Lily's favorite part. The giddy swirl of dancers mimicking the movements of snow in the air. And then, as the music swelled, a leap into the air ... outstretched arms ... and snow. Paper snow shooting from their fingertips. Paper snow filling the air, covering the stage.

I knew this was my cue to leave. I knew I needed a head start for the last piece of the puzzle. But I had to stand there and watch. I had to see Lily – holding her brother's prize possession, full of hot chocolate from her grandfather, guided here by friends and family alike. If this didn't make her happy, maybe I never could. If this didn't bring her back from the darker places into the more colorful ones, maybe I was too late.

But I wasn't too late. Even from the highest balcony, I could see.

With the stealth of a chimney dropper, I tiptoed from

the theater. I turned my phone back on and sent out a group message.

It's a wonderful life.

I knew the last part of the plan would be the most challenging. But I was wrong in diagnosing what the challenges would actually be.

I had thought Santa would be the problem, but it ended up being the elf.

I met Lily's creepy Great-Uncle Sal in a Macy's changing room. I was wearing my street clothes. He was wearing his Santa uniform.

"We have to do this quickly," he said. "You go out there, you do your thing with Lily, and then you get right back here, okay?"

"Fine," I told him, wishing I'd rented my own suit. (I'd called three places the night before; they were all out.) "I'll just wait in the changing room next door, and you can pass the suit through the curtain."

"No, no," he said, starting to shimmy out of his Santa top. "Right here, right now."

The changing room wasn't big enough for the two of us. I could smell Santa's sweat. I could feel it in the air.

I had known from my last interaction with this Santa that he wouldn't be wearing an undershirt under his Santa jacket. But still, knowing it and seeing it were two very different things. Because being forced to touch Santa's large, hairy belly to get an envelope from Lily was nothing compared to seeing it in the fleshiest fleshly flesh. Not only did it look like a hirsute whale rising upright from a skin-colored ocean, but there was also a tattoo – two words – YES, VIRGINIA. Only, the fold of Santa's tummy cut off the last two letters.

I took Santa's coat and threw it over my head, if only to cover my eyes. It was far too big for me, but that was okay – I wasn't going for accuracy here, only effect. When I got it in place, I looked over and saw Santa had removed his red pants, revealing candy-cane-patterned boxer shorts.

Santa caught me looking and murmured, "You like?"

I grabbed the pants out of his hands and quickly tried to put them on. But in focusing on speed, I took my eye off of balance, and as I got my second leg in, I began to wobble . . . and found myself falling right into Santa's chest.

"Ho ho ho!" he cried, delighted.

"No no no!" I cried back.

I tried to pull my pants up and pull my body back, but I didn't do it fast enough. Because right when I leaned to clear the second pant leg over my sneaker, the door to the changing room whipped open and an elf shouted, "WHAT DO YOU THINK YOU'RE DOING?!?"

And not just any elf –

Santa's number one helper.

We'd scuffled a year ago, and here we were again.

"OUTRAGE!" he called out. "OUTRAGE IN CHANGING ROOM FOUR!"

"Desmond," Santa said. "Calm down."

"HE'S STEALING YOUR SUIT!"

154

"He's borrowing it."

"THAT'S NOT ALLOWED!"

I got the pants in place, then felt in the coat's pocket. As promised, there was a beard inside.

I was about to grab Santa's hat when the elf stepped in and body-blocked me.

"SANTA!" he chided.

"Go," Santa said.

It took me a second to understand he was talking to me.

"There's a spare hat under the sleigh," he added.

I made a move to leave. I just had to get past the elf.

"I WILL NOT TOLERATE NAUGHTINESS!" he screamed. "SECURITY! *SECURITY!*"

Lily was going to be here any moment. I had to push past. I was getting ready to do it – run right over the elf. But then Santa stretched out his naked arms, grabbed the elf by his shoulders, and pulled him into a kiss.

My path was clear. I bolted.

As I passed the big changing room mirror, I threw on the beard. It wasn't my size, but it would do.

"SANTA, IT WAS ALWAYS YOU!" Desmond cried out from changing room number four as I headed out to my throne.

Benny was waiting for me in this floor's Santa's village to perform what might have been the most dangerous, riskiest role of the day. For the next ten minutes, he had the hazardous job of pretending to be a Macy's intern and telling parents that this Santa was on a pee break and that they should try the Santa on the second floor if they needed immediate attention. He didn't even have a Macy's badge – just a clipboard and a stern expression. ("People never say no when you're carrying a clipboard," he assured me. "If it was enough to get me backstage for Adele, it's enough to enable your Sant-o-mime.")

Sal's Santa station was at the back of a sleigh. I reached under and found a full spare outfit, and grabbed the hat. There wasn't any mirror, so I used my phone to check myself out and put everything in place. I was so focused on this that I didn't notice the little boy in front of me until he said, "Santa, why are you taking a selfie?"

"I was just waiting for you to show up," I said, all while thinking, *How did you get past Benny, kid?*

(Answer: Kids don't give a shit about clipboards.)

Without a moment's hesitation, the boy climbed right onto my lap and sat down on my thigh.

Fine, I thought. *We're going to do this.*

"What's your name?" I asked.

"Max."

"And have you been naughty or nice this year?"

I could see him do the mental calculations, then figure out which answer led to presents.

"Nice," he said decisively.

"Good. That's really all I need to know. Have a merry Christmas!"

But Max wasn't budging.

"Tanner in my class says you're not real," he said.

"I'm right here," I pointed out. But that didn't feel right. If it wasn't a lie, it felt like a dodge. I owed Max better.

"Look, Max," I said. "The thing to remember – what I really want you to remember – is that it doesn't matter whether I actually live at the North Pole or whether I'm the one who brings you presents every Christmas Eve. People like Tanner are going to tell you I'm pretend, and then when you get older, people like Tanner are going to tell you other things are pretend. But you know what to say to that? *So what*. That's what you tell them. Because at the end of the day, it doesn't matter whether the story's true or not. What matters is the care that's been put into the story. The love. If something is pretend, that usually means someone has taken the time to build a story for you to live in. And building stories takes *a lot* of work. And, yes, there will come a time when you'll see the story isn't true. But the intentions behind it? Completely true. The love behind it? Also true."

Max's eyes had glazed over a little. When I was done, he blinked and asked, "But what about presents?"

"You'll get them. And they will come from people who love you. Which means much more than having the presents come from some arbitrary guy with reindeer at his disposal."

Max seemed satisfied with that.

And so did the girl standing behind him.

I hadn't noticed Lily come in, I had been so focused on Max.

"Why, hello," I said.

She'd put away Joey and the red Moleskine and the $12.21 Macy's gift card. The only thing in her hand was the card I'd written her, with its two words:

Happy Anniversary.

"Run along now," I murmured to Max. He took the cue and took off toward Benny, who was waiting to usher him out to his parents.

"Hi," Lily said.

"Hi," I said.

"You're dressed as Santa," she observed.

"There's no getting one past you, is there?"

"For me."

"Let's just say this is not a situation that would have ever happened if I'd never met you."

Lily took out her phone and grinned. "I'm sorry, but I have to do this."

She took a picture. But I was really the one who wanted to have a picture – not of me in a Santa suit, but of her seeing me in a Santa suit. She looked like someone who believed I was real.

"Happy anniversary," I told her, repeating the two words I'd written in her card.

"Happy anniversary."

"Now come here, you. We only have a short time before another kid gets around Benny."

"I'm not sitting on your lap," Lily said.

I patted the bench of the sleigh. "I left you some room here."

She put down her bag and sat next to me. She was still a little out of breath from running around.

"So," I said, "tell me about your year."

In response, she began to cry.

I wasn't expecting this, but I wasn't not expecting it either. I knew this had been inside her. I just hadn't known if she'd ever let it out. I was grateful that Santa decided to dress softly, because it made it easier for me to pull her close, easier to hold her there.

"It's okay," I told her.

She shook her head. "No, it's not okay."

I took her chin in my hand. Made her look past the beard, into my eyes.

"No. I mean that it's okay that it's not okay."

"Oh. Okay."

What an idiot Santa is for flying around alone. Because who would want to travel the world without another person's heartbeat beside him?

"We have to talk to each other," I said. "There will always be a part of us that's on a chase, but there has to be another part that knows where our home base is. Our North Pole, as it were. Even if it doesn't really exist, we can still get there if we agree that it exists. I love you, and it's driving me crazy to see you so upset. I want to fix it, and I know I can't. But what I want to do is rewrite the whole world so you can fix it. I want to come up with a story that all the world will choose to celebrate, and in it, the people we love will never get sick, and the people we love will never be sad for long, and there would be unlimited frozen hot chocolate. Maybe if it were up to me I wouldn't have the whole world collectively believe in Santa Claus, but I would definitely have them collectively believe in *something*, because there is a messed-up kind of beauty in the way we can all bend over backward to make life seem magical when we want to. In other words, after giving it some thought, I think that reality has the distinct potential to completely suck, and the way to get around that is to step out of reality from time to time and find something a little more enjoyable with someone you completely, unadulteratedly enjoy. In my life, that's you. And if it takes dressing up like Santa to get that across to you, then so be it."

"But what if it's all just pretend?" Lily asked.

"I think that maybe by pretending, we find out more about who we really are. Not that I want to be Santa. But I guess I want to be the guy who goes through all kinds of psychological horrors to dress up as Santa for you."

"Psychological horrors?"

As if on cue, there was a commotion from outside our village. An elf's voice, loud and clear: "WE HAVE AN INTRUDER ON THE PREMISES!"

I turned to Lily. "Remember what I said before? Well, I stand by the coming-up-with-stories part, and the I-love-you part, and the dressing-up-as-Santa-to-make-you-happy part. But the maybe-we-shouldn't-chase-so-much part? I'm rethinking it, since now would be an *excellent* time to make chase."

"Can we take the sleigh?"

"I fear the sleigh is bolted to the floor. We may have to make a much more pedestrian exit. You game?"

Lily sprang up, wiped her eyes, and jumped from the sleigh. "I'm so game."

We found the door and took it. Then I found a men's room and divested myself of Santa's finery – I didn't want to seem like a leftover from SantaCon, wandering the streets in search of the bridge or tunnel to take me home. I left Sal's outfit dangling from the back of a door, then texted him a photo of its location.

When I emerged from the men's room, I caught Lily jotting in the red Moleskine. When she saw me, she shut it.

"Shall we?" I asked.

"Where to?"

"I was thinking *It's a Wonderful Life*? Seven o'clock showing at Film Forum? I have some cookies in my bag."

The look on her face was priceless. Sweet Lily was wondering how to break it to me.

"Cookies from Levain," I added. "I don't quite know how they do it, but they're ninety percent sugar, ninety percent butter, and maybe six percent flour. In other words, we should eat as many of them as possible while we're still young and our bodies can take it."

We got to the door to Herald Square. An unmiraculous Thirty-Fourth Street beckoned.

"Remember," I said to Lily. "Anything we want. Any way we want our story to go. This is not the time for reality.

161

Reality can return in January, if it has to. But now – the city is ours for the making."

I thought we'd rush forth then – but Lily stayed where she was, shoppers pushing past us both.

"Dash?" she said. "You do realize you said it, right? Twice."

"Really?" I replied. "I thought I only said 'unadulteratedly' once."

Her face clouded. "That's not what I meant."

I looked her right in the eye.

"I'll say it again right now if you'd like. In fact, let me let these strangers know." I started addressing the people pushing by us. "Sir, I love Lily. Ma'am, I happen to love Lily. I love Lily – I love Lily – I LOVE LILY! I am a Santa-dressing lovelorn fool for Lily! If loving Lily is a crime, then proclaim me guilty as charged! Shall I go on?"

Lily nodded.

"I love Lily more than you people love Christmas! I love Lily more than Mr. Macy loves your consumer dollars! I love Lily so much it should be put in shop windows! My love for Lily is higher than the GNP of most industrialized nations! I love – "

Lily put her hand on my arm. "Okay. Stop."

"Are we on the same page now?"

"I believe we are."

"And even though there's no mistletoe in sight, may I kiss you in the middle of this crowded department store entrance?"

"Yes."

So there we were. That completely obnoxious pair of teenagers making out in the doorway of a major department store, eliciting stares and curses from passersby and not caring one bit.

"Happy anniversary," I said, pulling back.

"Happy anniversary," she said, pulling in.

Then, hand in hand, we plunged into the night.

We still had four days until Christmas, and it was time to fill them with the right story.

10
LILY

Rawkettes a-Leaping

Monday, December 22nd

Christmas can go fudge itself, because I already have what I want: Dash.

I could feel the faint light of morning sun on my face, but before I opened my eyes, I wanted to enjoy the rise and fall of his breathing against my chest, his warm body pressed against mine.

Yesterday, arguably the best day of my life not including any *Star Wars* movie opening days, Dash and I had declared our love for each other. When Dash took me home last night, we cuddled by the fire, gazing at our beautiful tree-baby, Oscar. I told him how much I loved him. "I love your obscure books and moody music and even your terrible cookies. I love your kindness. I love you for loving Christmas, despite yourself. For me." I'd been holding it in for so long, and needed to talk it all out. "When did you know you loved me?" I asked Dash.

He said, "There wasn't an actual moment. Don't look so

disappointed. It was more a gradual realization. A knowing of how much sweeter my life was for having you in it. Sofia telling me how much lighter and happier I seemed since knowing you."

I wasn't jealous of Sofia at all anymore. At least, not in terms of Dash. I'd never not be jealous of her Euro-elegance and her un-American, rational relationship with sugary foods. "Did you tell Boomer and Sofia you loved me before you told me?"

"Didn't need to. Apparently everyone else knew before I did."

"We have an anniversary! I love us for that! I love you for telling me you loved me on it!"

"You didn't remember, did you?"

"I didn't," I confessed. My December mind has traditionally been so caught up in Christmas it hadn't even occurred to me that my own romance could now be included in important holiday dates. "Which Nicholas Sparks book do you think we as a couple are the most like? Say *The Notebook*!"

Dash's dreamy blue eyes turned icy blue-gray. "Don't even joke about something like that."

I hadn't been joking.

I asked, "Am I ruining the moment by overtalking it?"

"Yes. Let's talk it out silently."

And we did, through many, many kisses, before we fell asleep on the living room floor – fully clothed, fully exhausted.

For now, there was waking up next to each other to savor. Drool dribbled onto my arm and I fluttered my eyes open. Darnsicles! It was Boris I was spooning, and not Dash. My waking disappointment was silly. I was actually doubly blessed. I already had what I wanted, this year *and* last. Dash, and a dog. My red Moleskine runneth over.

Dash lay on the other side of Boris, half-awake. Dash had already gotten what he wanted for Christmas, too. His mom went away on her annual holiday vacation, and she didn't insist Dash stay at his dad's while she was away, so Dash didn't need to lie to them by saying he was staying at the other's apartment. What Dash wanted most was to have his home to himself. He could have that, later. For right now, he was all mine.

My heart was still exploding with exhilaration. I loved a boy! He loved me back! He baked me cookies! That hadn't made me sick!

I knew I had serious competition for his affection. Dash greedily eyed the bookcase next to Oscar. Instead of saying "Good morning," I asked him, "Why do you love books so much?" It wasn't a hostile question, like I was jealous of those firm, colorful spines that beheld so much wonder between their . . . pages. I was genuinely curious.

Dash said, "From the time I was a baby, my mom took me to the library at least once a week. Librarians were like Mary Poppins to me. They always knew how to match a book to my mood or to whatever I was going through at the time. I could always find peace in books."

"And escape?"

"Escape, sure. But it wasn't so much about getting away, as going to. You can go anywhere in a book. Books are adventure. Knowledge. Possibility. Magic."

I couldn't believe my beloved, snarly Dash had spoken such blasphemy. I propped myself halfway up from the floor and looked down at his amazing face. (And beheld Boris's amazing smoosh face next to Dash's, too. I was such a lucky girl!) "You believe in magic?" I said to Dash. Those two faces. My boyfriend and my dog. They were my magic.

"Yes," said Dash. Then, solemnly, he added, "But please don't ever tell anyone I said that."

"I heard it!" squealed Langston as he walked through the living room toward the kitchen. He singsonged, "*Dash believes in magic. Must be love!*"

Benny followed my brother into the room. Seeing Dash and me lying on the floor together, Benny did a mock bump and grind against Langston's hip. To me, Benny said, "Boyfriend staying over now? You're lucky Mami and Papi are still in Connecticut!" He looked at Dash, then back at Langston. "Should we beat Dash up now or later?"

"We're nice to Dash now," said Langston with a sigh.

"*¡Ñoña es!*" said Benny, which I believe was Puerto Rican for "No fucking way."

"It's love, I guess," Langston said with a sneer.

Benny said, "*¡Diantre!* Is it too soon to give the Christmas present?"

Langston shrugged. "If you must." He turned to Dash. "You may thank us for letting you open this now instead of later, in front of your girlfriend's parents."

Dash said nothing.

"Ingrate," said Langston.

Benny stepped to the pile of Christmas presents and took out a box covered in multicolored gift paper from the Strand. He tossed the box to Dash. Dash unwrapped. It was clearly a box set of books, so I didn't know why Dash's face turned so red. He held up the box set for me to see: the Collected Works of D. H. Lawrence.

"*¡Feliz Navidad!*" said Benny.

I didn't know what about D. H. Lawrence could cause such an embarrassed face from my boyfriend (and I'd surely be Googling immediately after to find out). "Be sexy, be safe, dear literary Dash!" said Langston, laughing.

"Said from the person moving to Hoboken," retorted Dash. "Sexy. Safe. Hoboken. Hmmm, which of these words does not belong?"

"HOBOKEN?" I yelled. The reaction was so instinctive, I didn't have time to process that Boris was lying next to me. Hearing my cry, Boris immediately jumped to his feet and pummeled Benny, the least familiar person to him in the room, to the ground.

"Did I forget to tell you the location part of our new apartment?" Langston asked me.

"Willful nondisclosure," I accused him. But I knew I was equally at fault. I'd been so upset by Langston telling me he was moving out that I'd neglected to ask where.

Langston said, "Manhattan and Brooklyn are way too expensive. And Queens and the Bronx are just too far from downtown."

"*Hola!*" said Benny. "*Ayúdame!*"

"Heel," I commanded Boris, who then unpinned Benny.

"Breakfast," said Dash.

"I'll make some," said Langston. "You're welcome."

"Not with you," said Dash. He took my hand. "We have a morning date with Mrs. Basil E. She wants to discuss plans for her Christmas-night party." The excitement on Dash's face was clear. For a guy who used to hate Christmas, he'd certainly turned over a new leaf. Or a new holly. Gift idea! Mistletoe-laden books. Dash pulled my hand to his face and placed a kiss on my palm. If he'd had them available, I believe he would have sprinkled the kiss with candy cane bits.

Dash believed in magic. Dash loved Christmas. Dash loved *me*!

I am indeed so shallow that I was much too concerned with the love in my heart and the promise of breakfast to dwell on my brother moving to godforsaken Hoboken. Whatever. Go already, Langston. What did I care? I had Dash. My real worry was that my relationship with my boyfriend was actually a ruse for Dash to spend more time with his real true love, my octogenarian great-aunt.

Langston told Dash, "I liked you better when you were snarly."

Dash said, "You didn't like me at all."

"Exactly," said Langston.

It pained me to admit it. But I did. "Grandpa looks great," I said to Mrs. Basil E. privately as she ushered us from her drawing room to her dining room for breakfast. He walked ahead of us with Dash, and there was a spring in his step again, and his eyes were sparkling with his old cheer and mischief when he'd greeted us.

Mrs. Basil E. said, "It was wearing on him, all the care you've been giving him. He doesn't want to be a burden, and he felt guilt all the time."

"He's not!" I said, about to defend our health care situation, until Mrs. Basil E. shushed me.

"He belongs to me, too," she said. "And you need to be young and taking care of yourself. I'm interviewing home health aide candidates next week to pick up the slack with Grandpa's needs."

Somehow I felt like I'd let Grandpa down. "But I can do the job," I said.

"I know you can, dear. But for now, your family would like your job to go back to being a teenager."

"And dog walker."

"If you insist."

A glorious breakfast spread was set out on the dining table. Eggs, bagels, coffee, juice, fruit salad, and plenty of Dash's favorite, yogurt. We sat down to dig in.

Mrs. Basil E. told me, "Have some of the lox on

your bagel, Lily Bear. I had it brought down from Barney Greengrass this morning. It's the best."

Often when Mrs. Basil E. instructs me to eat something on her table that once had eyes, I politely put some of the cooked flesh on my plate and move it around there, but never eat it. This time I didn't. I said, "I'd like to not be called Lily Bear anymore, please. And I'm a vegetarian."

"You don't even eat fish?" asked Mrs. Basil E. I will never understand why meat eaters always ask that question when I say I'm a vegetarian. If she next asked where I got my protein, I'd be tempted to toss my plate at the wall like the ungrateful-but-sick-of-that-question not-Lily-Bear that I am.

"No, I don't eat fish," I said sweetly.

"Why didn't you say so before?" said Mrs. Basil E. "No use wasting this glory on your dull palate."

She placed an additional slice of lox on Grandpa's bagel. "Good!" said Grandpa between bites.

"And she's no longer our bear," Mrs. Basil E. said to Grandpa. They shook their heads sadly. "Is this your doing?" Mrs. Basil E. asked Dash.

Dash said, "I had nothing to do with it. Lily's been a vegetarian since kindergarten."

Mrs. Basil E. gasped. "No one ever told me!"

I've told her a million times. I've been to vegetarian restaurants with her. She's sharp as a tack, my great-aunt – but, like Grandpa, she's getting more forgetful. It's worrisome. Right then I made up my mind. If my parents moved to Connecticut, I'd accept Mrs. Basil E.'s invitation to live at her house, with her and Grandpa. They needed me. Five stories of townhouse was more than enough room for us all. And Boris. Five stories of stairs would be a problem for Grandpa. But we'd figure out a way to keep him mobile.

Dash said, "The bagels are delicious."

"Of course they are," said Mrs. Basil E. "I don't trifle with subpar carbs."

"So how can we help you with your Christmas party?" Dash asked Mrs. Basil E.

"You show up," she said, like it was obvious.

"I thought you asked us here because you need our help. We'd be glad to help," Dash offered.

"I hire help for my parties, young man." She looked at him, then at me, then back at Dash again. "So it's love now?"

"One-year anniversary!" I said proudly. A lark of a red Moleskine dare had led me to this wondrous boy. Now here we were a year later. Stronger than ever. Love officially declared.

"Hand me the list, brother," Mrs. Basil E. said to Grandpa.

Grandpa reached into his pocket and extracted a folded piece of paper, which he handed to Mrs. Basil E. She unfolded the paper and pressed down the creases to straighten it, and then she handed the piece of paper to Dash. "If you're to be official with Lily, here is the list of holidays, in descending order of importance. My Christmas-night party is at the top, obviously."

I couldn't believe Dash had gotten a copy of the List. Usually prospective members of our family didn't get it until they were engaged to one of our relatives. *And* registered at a wedding gift store that met Mrs. Basil E.'s approval.

"I don't understand," said Dash.

"It's the attendance sheet," Grandpa told Dash, laughing. "Good luck, kid."

"It's no such thing," Mrs. Basil E. chided. "It's merely a list of holidays you are expected to celebrate with us if you are part of this family, ranked by order of importance. The asterisks denote optional holidays, and the footnotes indicate floating holidays that you are allowed to attend with your own family on a rotating basis."

Dash scanned the list and then looked up, askance. "Canadian Thanksgiving is a footnote holiday?"

"Not to Canadians," said Mrs. Basil E.

Dash said, "My father will be relieved. He's Canadian."

A shocked silence fell over the breakfast table. Finally, almost feeling betrayed, I said, "You never told me your father is Canadian."

"Does it matter?" Dash asked.

"Of course it matters!" said Grandpa. But it was a defensive reaction. We all knew it didn't matter.

The shock was, we all knew about Dash's dad. "But your dad's –" I didn't want to come out and say it. *Such a rhymes-with-ick*.

Mrs. Basil E. spared me having to speak the harsh language aloud. She snapped, "Not all Canadians are nice,

Lily. Don't be so naïve. Dashiell, we'll take custody of you on Canadian Thanksgiving. You may direct your father to me if he has any concerns."

"I love this family!" Dash said, beaming.

Mrs. Basil E. and I nodded knowingly at each other. We knew Dash meant he loved us the most. We knew he'd choose us for Canadian Thanksgiving.

Dash's beam of happiness flooded my heart with joy, once again. He'd given me so much happiness yesterday.

But I owned Christmas. Everyone knew that. I couldn't let Dash out-Christmas me in romantic gestures. I wanted to shout out my love for him from the rooftops. And now that I knew Dash was part Canadian, I knew exactly which rooftop I wanted to shout it from.

"How's Mr. Zamboni?" I asked Grandpa.

Grandpa's a ladies' man, but he hasn't acquired any new girlfriends since his heart attack. His bromances are still going strong, though. He has a standing weekly date with his buddies at our local Italian pork store, where the guys meet to sip espresso and play backgammon. Since I was a kid, I always referred to Grandpa's friends by the names of their businesses instead of their proper names. Mr. Dumpling, the retired Chinese restaurant owner, prefers tea over coffee. Mr. Borscht, the retired Polish deli owner, bets too hard on his backgammon prowess and has lost many rolls of quarters to his pals as a result. (The Żubrówka – bison grass vodka – that he adds to his sparkling water might also contribute to his losses.) Mr. Zamboni, the aging-but-not-yet-retired real estate developer, has gone gluten-free, so no pastries for him at their games anymore, but he goes "nuts" for the gluten-free peanut butter cookies I regularly make for him. Mr. Zamboni loves the cookies so much that he's long been saying he owes me a favor, which I was ready to cash in on.

Despite my name for him, Mr. Zamboni isn't really involved in the ice-skating business. But a few years ago he built a new condo building on the far west side of Manhattan, overlooking the High Line, with a communal rooftop that's converted to an ice-skating rink during the winter. Personally, I prefer to pay a few Andrew Jacksons for a skate session at Rockefeller Center or Wollman Rink, but some people need to spend several million on a condo to get that Christmas ice-skating feeling, I guess. They like their holidays cold with exclusivity and privilege. But their obscene wealth was beneficial to me, today at least.

I gave Dash the address and then told him to meet me there at seven p.m. I needed the afternoon to myself to take care of the details. Invitations. Food. Performers. Pyrotechnics.

When Dash arrived at the lobby entrance to Mr. Zamboni's building that night, the first thing he asked was, "Aren't you cold in that?" The weather was indeed very chilly, but I wore thick tights under my Rockette Christmas outfit – a red crushed-velvet dancer's A-line dress, falling just above my knees, tight at the waist with a sash, trimmed in faux white fur along the bottom hem and the plunging neckline.

I said no, and gave Dash a kiss. I was a little cold, admittedly, but my heart was so very warm. Would I ever get over this flush of happiness at the sight of him? Probably never.

Next, Dash asked, "Are we going to the High Line?" It was one of his favorite places in Manhattan – an elevated train track on the West Side that was turned into a beautiful garden and park area.

"Sort of," I said.

I took his hand in mine and led him to the elevator. Before I pressed the Up button, I untied the white sash from my waist. "Blindfold?" I asked Dash. I wanted his first sight of our party to be a surprise.

"This isn't some bondage party, is it?" Dash asked. He must have started one of those D. H. Lawrence books. Oh yes, I Googled.

"No. But thank you for thinking me capable of such a kinky idea."

I placed the sash over Dash's eyes and tied it at the back of his head. Then I swiped the keycard that would allow us to gain entrance to the elevator and the top floor of the building.

"This isn't, like, a surprise party?" Dash asked, worried, as the elevator went up. "My birthday's not in December."

"It's not."

"I mean, people aren't going to jump out from behind

bushes on a rooftop garden and scare me? I'm all for a good fright. But not in a tall building."

"Relax."

The elevator opened, and I led Dash into the staging area, where benches and tables were set up, with a tented dome built overhead to resemble an igloo. The music was loud and the party was already in full swing. I could see Boomer and Sofia skating together, holding hands. Edgar Thibaud and his argyle coat, aggressively speed skating like he'd just downed a case of Red Bulls. Our guests of honor, none of whom I knew personally, were also out on the rink. Some of them were good skaters, but more of them were holding on to the outer rink rail for dear life. Their many canvas bags filled with books were lined up alongside their street shoes and boots in the igloo area.

I untied the sash and told Dash, "Behold. A Christmas ice-skating. With all your favorite people!"

Dash looked at the rink, then back at me. "The only people I recognize on the rink are Boomer and Sofia. And Edgar. Ugh."

I said, "The rest are librarians. My cousin Mark at the Strand knows about a Listserv for librarians, so he posted the invitation there for them. You are literally surrounded by book people tonight. Literally. Get it?"

Dash winced at my lame joke, but brightened at the sight of the refreshment stand at the other end of the igloo. "Is that a hot chocolate station?" Dash asked.

"Sure is! I hired Jacques Torres Chocolate to cater

the party with hot chocolates and regular chocolates and chocolate chip cookies and –"

"People are going to be in a diabetic coma by the time they leave."

"Hopefully! That's how we know it's a good party. Mrs. Basil E. always says, 'The worse people feel the next day, the better the party.'"

Dash smiled. Then frowned. "This must have cost a lot of money."

"Only the catering. And the talent. It's my pleasure."

I don't like to brag, but I'm quite wealthy. Not through my pauper academic parents, but because of my dog-walking business. My bank account has five numerals in it (barely), and that's before the decimal point. The money is supposed to be my college fund. I'd rather spend it on Christmas.

"The talent?" Dash said.

"You'll see," I said. I handed him his pair of skates. "Let's lace up."

"True confession. I'm not a very good skater."

"But you're part Canadian!"

"My love for Arcade Fire is all I got from the Canada gene."

I put my own skates on, then helped Dash with his. He stood up, wobbling, and I held on to him as we approached the rink. "You're not going to believe the view," I promised him.

I took his hand and led him to the rink. He really was a very bad skater. Over-cautious, nervous, wobbly, until we reached the edge, and he saw the view. The Manhattan skyline to the north, co-headlined by the Empire State Building and the Chrysler Building, and to the west, the Hudson River and New Jersey (whatever). Below us, the High Line. "Incredible," said Dash. "Even if the height kind of makes me want to throw up."

"Merry Christmas," I told him.

We barely had time for another kiss and to skate the loop of the rink before the talent arrived. They were there earlier than I'd originally planned, because the weather had turned from very cold to freezing, and drizzling, which meant freezing rain might be next, so I'd texted the entertainers to start immediately after Dash's arrival.

Edgar Thibaud skated to the middle of the rink like a pro hockey player. I'd hired him to emcee. He held up celebratory sparklers in each of his hands and announced, "Ladies, gentlemen, distinguished librarians. Please join me in welcoming . . . the Rawkettes!"

The Rawkettes are a punk rock dance troupe started by my great-uncle Carmine's dancer granddaughter, who decided to take all the experience from her failed Rockette auditions and use it to turn her stage act into a sideline more commensurate with her talent. The dancers in her group are also sci-fi fangirls, so for a while they were called the Spockettes and wore blue Rockette costumes designed like Starfleet uniforms, but after a lack of bookings, they recently changed their name to the Rawkettes, to try a new direction. This skate party was their first booking in their latest incarnation. Possibly their first booking ever.

"Is that Kerry-cousin?" Dash asked me as she took center stage with her troupe, all of them wearing "punk" outfits that looked more Ziggy Stardust than Sid Vicious. Lots of bright face glitter and gold-lamé 1970s-era pantsuits. I couldn't wait to commend Mrs. Basil E. Dash was indeed so worthy of receiving the List! He recognized and also knew to call Great-Uncle Carmine's granddaughter "Kerry-cousin," to distinguish her in our family language from "Carrie-aunt" and "Kharie-neighbor," and Cary Grant, whose name needs no quotations, and whose movies everyone adores.

"It is!" I said.

Edgar cued the music, and Kerry-cousin and her troupe began their dance interpretation of one of Dash's favorite songs – "Calamity Song" by the Decemberists. Not a band I particularly like, except during the month of December, but I do like how their lyrics make no sense. *Hetty Green / Queen of supply-side bonhomie bone-drab.*

Dash looked at me like, No! and I looked at him like, Oh heck, yes!

It was amazing. All of Dash's favorite things in one place. The High Line! Librarians! Hot chocolate! The Decemberists!

And then the rain really started to fall – in mean, icy pellets. "Now!" I beseeched Kerry-cousin. I wanted the Rawkettes to hurry the night's grand finale before the rain did it for them. And so, holding Santa-present satchels, the Rawkettes skated around the rink, weaving in and out of librarians, and me and Dash, and Sofia and Boomer, and

180

Edgar, throwing glitter into the air from inside their satchels. I'd wanted the night to end with an explosion of crystal color on the ice.

And for a moment, it was indeed a magical world of color, just like at Disneyland. The ice twinkled in pinks, greens, purples, golds, and silvers. But too quickly, I realized: The glitter shouldn't have been twinkling. The sprays of glitter should have been more iridescent, like soft snow flurries.

Why was everyone suddenly falling down? Was it the freezing rain, or the glitter?

"What kind of glitter is this?" I shouted to Kerry-cousin as she weaved between Dash and me. Glitter, glitter, glitter – everywhere there was glitter as the Rawkettes tossed handfuls on the rink like fairy dust.

"Craft store glitter!" she said. "You said to spare no expense, so I didn't!"

I picked up a handful of glitter from the ice. It was not the cosmetic kind of glitter, like Kerry-cousin had on her face. This glitter was on a Martha Stewart level of fancy, made of finely ground glass, the size and shape of small pebbles. This craft store glitter was not fairy dust at all, but thousands of tiny, sharp, lethal weapons strewn across ice. And it was causing a free fall of skaters on the rink, taking hard knocks down onto the ice.

Boomer flew by us – "Whee!" – and then took a nasty fall on the glitter. Dash leaned over to help him up just as another librarian took a fall, and the blade of her skate made a direct slice on Dash's face.

"My eye!" Dash cried out.

"My knee!" someone else shouted.

"I think I broke my wrist," said another voice.

It all happened so fast. One minute the Rawkettes were performing while librarians happily skated around them, and the next, there was a triage scene on the rink and emergency medics trying to maneuver stretchers across the ice, passing over streaks of blood from so many blade wounds. It was Chaos on Glitter Ice. A massacre of librarians.

As Dash was wheeled away to the ambulance, his wounded eye covered in bloody gauze, his hands already bruised and sliced from all the other skaters that had fallen on him, I told him, "I'm so sorry, Dash! I'll call your dad and let him know you're on the way to the hospital."

"Don't throw glitter in the wound, Lily," said Dash.

Kerry-cousin handed me an invoice. "You still owe me a hundred bucks."

I couldn't have felt worse. I was responsible for a small army of librarians – the nicest people in the world – being taken away in ambulances from a party designed to celebrate them. I'd mortally wounded my boyfriend.

The Lily who loved Christmas had just ruined it.

11
DASH

Don't Fear the Piper

Monday, December 22nd

'Twas three nights before Christmas and all through the hospital, not a creature was stirring . . . except for a half-dozen librarians on painkillers.

Because we'd all come in together from The Great Glitterskating Massacre, we were sharing a room in New York-Presbyterian. While I didn't know any of the librarians, they all knew each other – the skate-off had been an add-on to their usual pre-holiday NYC bender. There is something a little disturbing but mostly remarkable about seeing a bunch of librarians become completely unshelved, and in the close quarters of our medical confinement, I was getting to see all this up close . . . albeit only through one eye. Although it hadn't been a direct hit, the blade had gotten close enough to my cornea that they wanted me to wear a patch for protection as everything healed. Unfortunately, I'd taken a look in a mirror before they'd patched it up, and the eyeball looked like every vessel within it had burst, as if I'd stayed awake for a year straight without remembering to blink. Had I been auditioning to play a demon spawn in a Christmas pageant, I would have been a shoo-in. (Once bandaged, I was more of a shoo-in for Christmas Pirate #3.)

I'd gotten a text from my father saying he was "on his way" – but that had been two hours ago, which led me to wonder which way he was taking. In the meantime, my guardians were the Page-Turn Posse.

"'Santa Can't Feel His Face'!" Kevin from Kalamazoo (injury requiring neck brace and morphine) called out. "I've never related to that song as much as I relate to it now!"

"Santa needs to redecorate this room!" Jack from Providence (dislocated shoulder) added. It didn't surprise me that the drab hospital decor offended his sensibilities – he was dressed in the most elaborate Krampus sweater I'd ever seen, and bright neon blue pants that could have just as easily been leggings. "And Santa also needs a double . . ." He reached into his Marc Jacobs bag and pulled out a thermos, a cocktail shaker, and six cocktail glasses. "Voila!"

"Make mine a triple!" Chris, who'd arrived with Jack, but was from somewhere in New York, called out. (He had only a few bruises, but wanted to keep the rest of us company.)

"I'd settle for a double," I said.

All the librarians turned their heads to me in a collective shush.

"I'm afraid you have to survive library school, put up with the general public on a daily basis, and endure several years of budget cuts in order to deserve these drinks," Chris told me kindly. "But someday, Dash, all this will be yours! We know how to spot 'em, and you're a young, temporarily one-eyed librarian in the rough!"

They all toasted me then. And even though I was injured and about to face my father, I felt sufficiently cheered. I knew this wasn't the way Lily had wanted me to get it, but it was still, I was sure, what she had wanted me to get out of the evening.

I raised the paper cup of water the orderly had left me.

"Here's to the glitter that brought us together," I toasted. "All that glitters may not be gold, but sometimes glitter is much more fun than gold. And to Lily, for trying her best, even if it ended up injuring us considerably."

"To Lily!" they called out.

Jack was readying another toast when my father came barreling into the room.

"There you are!" my father said in a tone that made it sound as if I'd been hiding from him.

"Exactly where I was supposed to be," I replied.

From the way he was dressed (suit, tie, *eau de* Bombay Sapphire), I could tell I'd pulled him from a party. From his timing, I could tell that the pull hadn't been an urgent one.

"Did I interrupt your festivities?" I asked.

"Yes," my father replied. "In *Philadelphia*."

I stood corrected. And for a moment, I pictured him riding frantically in a cab, desperate to get to his son in the hospital. It was a touching image.

"Come on," my father said, impatient. "Leeza is waiting in the car. Get your stuff."

Okay, I thought. *That's the way it is.*

I started to gather my things, and my father started to leave the room.

"Not so fast," Jack said, putting his drink down on a gurney.

"Who are you?" my father asked.

"Doesn't matter. For the next minute, I am going to be your gosh darn conscience. And I am going to inform you that it's standard operating procedure that when you're picking your kid up in the hospital, the first, second, and third things you say to him are all versions of *Are you okay?*"

"That patch on his eye?" Chris chimed in. "*Not* a fashion statement."

My father did not have the time or patience to be told what to do. As often happened with my mom, his defense was to go on the attack.

"Who do you think you are?" he gruffly challenged.

Kevin strode toward him and thrust out his drink so it sloshed a little in my father's direction. "We're librarians, sir. And we will not let you check out this future librarian unless you prove to us that you'll take good care of him when he's in your home."

It was interesting to see my father face off against a librarian in a neck brace. But even more interesting was seeing how all the librarians in the room clearly thought my father was in the wrong here. I needed that reality check,

186

because at this point in my life I was just too used to it.

"It's okay," I said to everyone in the room. "Dad, I'll meet you in the waiting room. See if you can get some extra bandages from the doctor because I'll have to change them in the morning, and we might as well get them for free here. Librarians, I will need all of your email addresses, since there's a party I want to invite you to, if you're still in town."

Everyone did as I asked. As the librarians scribbled down their emails on a back page of my journal, a text came through from Lily.

How are you doing? she asked. (We'd already had a very long I'm-so-sorry-You-have-no-reason-to-be-sorry exchange.)

About to be discharged, I replied. *Up for something tomorrow that doesn't involve depth perception?*

You name it, she replied.

I will, I promised.

But first I'd have to survive a night with my father.

Leeza's first words to me when I got into the car were, "Oh no, you poor baby!"

Good sentiment, unfortunate word choice.

The whole ride home, she fussed and fretted about my eye, and by the time we got to the apartment, I felt my father was more annoyed at her than he was at me. Which was quite an achievement.

In many ways, Leeza was not what I'd been expecting for a stepmother. For one, I was expecting someone closer to my own age. But Leeza was actually a year older than my mother – something that annoyed my mom to no end, because it was one thing to be left for a newer model and quite another to be left for someone with as much mileage as you had. (My mother shouldn't have told me this, but on a particularly dark pre-stepfather night when I was ten, she had.)

Along similar lines, I was relieved that Leeza and my dad hadn't wanted to have another kid – my father broadcast this fact at many dinner parties that I was at in my formative years. This meant my status was secure. But at the same time, it also confirmed that maybe I hadn't been entirely wanted in the first place. Because if my dad had experienced such a good time with me, wouldn't he have wanted to experience it again? (I knew it was more complicated than this, but emotionally, this was how it sometimes felt.)

My room in my father's apartment was maybe one-quarter bedroom and three-quarters storage for yoga equipment and odds and ends. Usually Leeza cleaned it out to make the ratio at least fifty-fifty before I arrived, but this time she hadn't had a chance.

"I'm sorry," she said, moving an exercise ball off the general area of my pillow. "If you want, I can get you some cleaner sheets. I changed them after you were here the last time – but I know that was months ago."

Mercifully, there wasn't any rebuke in her recitation of this fact. At least not until my father walked by and seized it.

"Yes, it hasn't escaped my attention that your presence has been scarce here, Dashiell," he said from the doorway.

188

"It's been that way for the whole year, no? About the same time you met Lily, if I'm not mistaken. I know what teenage hormones are like, but family is family, and it's about time you realized that."

"Now, now, dear," Leeza said, armfulling some yoga mats into the closet. "We love Lily."

"We love what we've seen of Lily," my father replied. "But I have to say – first, a year ago, she lands you in jail. And now she's landed you in the hospital. It makes me wonder whether Lily's the right kind of girl for you to be spending so much time with."

"Are you kidding me?" I said.

"I'm not kidding at all."

I stared him down with my one good eye. "You don't know Lily at all and you don't know *me* at all, so your observations, while delivered with conviction, are just so much horseshit to me, Dad."

My father grew bright red. "Now you look here, Dashiell –"

"No," I said, shaking my head. "Stop. You don't get to do this. You don't get to pass any judgment here."

"I am your father!"

"I am all too aware of that! And it's bad enough for you to treat me like an idiot. But don't you dare slander Lily in the process. It takes both her and Mom to balance out the seesaw with you on the other end."

My father laughed. "Ah – I knew your mother would factor into this. All of these things that she's told you –"

"No, *Dad*. These are the things I've told myself. Over and over and over again. Because, surprise! I am actually capable of coming to my own conclusions."

"Boys," Leeza interrupted, "I know it's been a really long day for all of us. And Dash needs rest after everything he's gone through. So why don't we call it a night?"

"I'm sorry," I said, "but I need to know if he even wants me here. Otherwise I can just go home."

"No, Dash," Leeza said sternly. "You are *not* staying alone tonight. Eventually, whatever drugs they gave you at the hospital are going to wear off and you're going to find it's not particularly comfortable to go to sleep with a bandaged eye. You need someone to take care of you."

I didn't tell her, but at that moment, she sounded exactly like my mom, in a way my mom would actually approve of.

"Listen to Leeza," my father said.

"There's no school tomorrow, right?" she went on. "Invite Lily over for breakfast. I'll make gingerbread pancakes."

"You'll *order* gingerbread pancakes," my father snarked.

"No," Leeza corrected, "I will *make* them. It'll be nice to have some people around who *deserve* them."

"Good lord, I know when I'm not wanted," my father huffed. "I'll see you in the morning, Dashiell."

"He loves you," Leeza said once he was gone.

"You shouldn't be the one telling me that," I replied.

"I know."

While she went out to the closet to get some new sheets, I texted Lily with the invitation to breakfast. It was late, so I wasn't expecting her to be up. But she responded right away, excited.

"Lily's on board for gingerbread pancakes," I told Leeza when she returned. Then I took the sheets out of her arms; I could make my own bed.

"Lovely!" she said with compensatory cheer. "Is there anything else I can do for you before I head to bed?"

Tell me why you're married to my father, I didn't say. *Tell me that when I make mistakes they're going to be my mistakes, not his mistakes.*

"I'm good," I told her.

She brought me a glass of water for my bedside anyway, and a few Tylenol. After she kissed me on the cheek good-night, she pulled back and considered me one more time.

"It's actually not a bad look for you. More bounty hunter than pirate, I'd say. Work it while you can."

I dug out my pajamas from a drawer.

"And Dash?" Leeza said from the doorway. I looked back up at her. "You're right about Lily. She's a keeper."

But why, I wondered as I began the long, long, somewhat tortured road to sleep, would she ever want to keep me, if paternity was destiny?

Tuesday, December 23rd

I hadn't told Lily about the gingerbread pancakes; she arrived with freshly baked gingerbread muffins. I was going to explain this coincidence to her, but I was interrupted by her crying out, "YOUR FACE!"

"What about my face?" I asked. "You can't honestly see it under all these bandages, can you? My goal is to haunt an opera house by the time I'm twenty-three."

"It's not funny!"

"Actually, it is. And I think in this case, we can agree that I get to be the one to determine the humor of the situation, no?"

I leaned in to kiss her. Because of the whole half-blind thing, my aim was a little off. But she was nice enough to correct my miscalculation in a rather satisfying manner.

"I may start pulling an Adam Driver," I warned her. "Wear a mask just for the fun of it. I mean, to prove that I'm badass and evil. That's a *Star Wars* reference, by the way, not a *Girls* reference."

"I got that one," Lily said. And I thought, *Voila! Now you're not thinking about my injury anymore!*

Before she could start drowning me in Apology Soup, I led her into the kitchen, where Leeza was over the griddle and my father was over the *Wall Street Journal*.

"Great minds think alike!" Leeza exclaimed when she saw the muffins.

"More like every goddamned thing nowadays is gingerbread for Christmas," my father added. "Don't get me wrong – I'm glad it's not *pumpkin*, for Christ's sake. But still. Gingerbread's hardly an original thought. If you ask me, I blame Starbucks."

"Nobody's asking you, dear," Leeza said lightly, taking out the muffins and putting them on a serving tray.

Within a few minutes, the pancakes were ready. Leeza had even made them in the shapes of ginger people. (It seemed strange to me to gender cookies.) What then followed was something that Lily was deeply unfamiliar with – familial silence. Every now and then one of us – even my father – would compliment the pancakes. But otherwise . . . nothing. Lily kept staring at my bandages, horrified. My father wouldn't stop reading his paper. Leeza smiled vaguely, as if there were invisible elves telling her gossip.

I imagined this was what every meal with Leeza and my dad was like. When it had been my dad and my mom, silence had meant a truce. Here, it was a default void.

Please may we not become like this, I wanted to say to Lily.

And maybe she got that, because when I looked back at her, she rolled her eyes.

I tried to roll my eyes back, forgetting for a second what a bad idea that was. The result was a not-so-gentle ice-pick-to-my-retina feeling.

I must have yelped, because both Lily and Leeza immediately asked if I was okay. Dad just looked annoyed.

"A-okay," I assured them. "But I just remembered – I need to change my bandage."

"I'll help you," Lily and Leeza said at the same time.

I can do it, I thought.

Then I thought, *But actually, I'd rather do it with Lily.*

"Thanks, Leeza," I said. "But I don't think I need that many hands to help out. I'm going to let Lily take this one."

We went to my room, where I got the gauze and tape from my backpack. Then we went into the bathroom, because even though I didn't particularly want to see it, I knew we should probably have a mirror handy. I took off my eye patch and then started to unravel what the doctor had done. But Lily stopped me, said, "Here, sit down. Let me."

I closed my eyes. I felt her peel the tape from my skin, as carefully as she could. I felt the gauze over my eye loosening, and loosening, and then finally falling away. Lily gasped a little at what she saw – the stitches, the bruising – but instead of saying anything, she kept working. We were silent now, yes, but it was a silence of concentration, of focus. Not just on her part, as she slowly put me back together. I was also feeling her fingers as they touched the side of my head. I was hearing her breathe. I was attuned to the most basic pulse of the moment. The gauze was put in place, kept in place. The eye patch went back on top, protecting the protection. A pat on my back – *All done, all good.*

I opened my eye.

"I hope I did that right," Lily said.

"If it were me, I probably would've wrapped up the wrong eye."

"There was some . . . glitter. Kind of embedded in the side of your face. I didn't know whether to take it out or leave it. I figure the doctor will do that next time?"

"Just adds to my street cred," I assured her. "Already balladeers are crafting legends about the boy known as Glitter Pirate and his way with the blades."

"I'm so –"

"Don't say it! It was no more your fault than it was Andrew Carnegie's fault for funding so many libraries, which led a century later to so many librarians on ice skates who were unprepared for glitter explosions. Anyway, I had a great time until the, you know, hospitalization. The Rawkettes knocked my socks off – which was no small feat, considering how laced up I was."

At this moment, Leeza called out, "Everything okay in there?"

Considering my father's comments about Lily's bad influence, I wanted to yell out something about champagne and a sponge bath – but I wasn't sure there'd be a way to explain the joke to Lily without hurting her feelings. So instead I yelled out, "All's well!" and then murmured to Lily, "We must get out of this apartment as quickly as humanly possible. In fact, forget human constraints – let's make like cheetahs. Or gazelles."

"Are you sure?" Lily asked, looking me in the eye.

"Why wouldn't I be sure?"

"I don't know. They made you pancakes."

"*She* made me pancakes. Mostly because she feels bad that he's such a jerk."

In certain circumstances, this would have been the point to say *Oh, he's not that bad*. But my father didn't merit those circumstances.

"The city awaits us!" I told Lily.

"Well, then," she said, putting all the supplies back in

my backpack, "we shouldn't keep it waiting."

We thanked Leeza about a dozen times each for the pancakes, and she asked us about a dozen times if we were sure we didn't want more.

"Leaving already?" my father said the minute he was done with his paper.

"Only two shopping days left!" I chirped, which sounded inane even to me.

"Well, what's the answer about Christmas? Will you be joining us or not?"

Only Leeza and Lily's presence prevented me from saying, "Not," and then walking away.

"I'm afraid I already have other plans," I said instead.

"What *plans*?" my father said skeptically.

I didn't want to tell him about Mrs. Basil E.'s party. Because she'd invited me in a way that I knew my father would never invite Lily. It didn't seem fair to put them on the same plane.

"I have plans with Lily," I answered, and let that be that.

"Wonderful!" Leeza said.

My father gave me a look to say, *Lily's not family.*

I tried to give him a look back that said, *She's better family to me than you are.*

I kissed Leeza on the cheek. She seemed surprised – this was not our goodbye ritual.

"I'll drop by after Christmas," I told her. "I promise."

"We'll be here!" she replied.

My father didn't get up from his seat.

"Bye, Dad," I said.

"Bye!" Lily echoed.

I was so relieved when we were out of there.

"So," Lily said when we got to the street, "what should we do? I have dog walking at three. But before that, I'm all yours."

"Well," I said, checking my watch, "it's a little too early for a Salty Pimp."

"Agreed. Maybe later. Do you need more caffeination?"

I shook my head. "I think it'll play with my head."

"So . . ."

"So . . ."

This is the funny thing about New York – there are so many things to do at all times of the day, but there are still moments when you have no idea which of them to do, and feel extra silly because you know there has to be *something* out there for you to do; your mind just hasn't found it yet.

"I didn't make any plans," Lily said apologetically. "After last night, I thought maybe I shouldn't."

"And I haven't made any plans. But we shouldn't let that tip us into planless despair."

"We could go help Langston and Benny pack."

"That may require too many visual cues."

"Oh. Sorry."

"Maybe we should just have an early Salty Pimp."

"I'm not even sure they're open at ten."

The whole city. We had the whole city! And yet . . .

"Do you hear that?" Lily asked. At first I didn't know what she meant. Then I focused not on my thoughts but on what was happening outside my thoughts – and I heard it.

"Is that bagpipes?" I asked.

"I think it's bagpipes," Lily said.

Then, as if to confirm our theory, a bagpiper rounded the corner. Then another. And another. Eleven times over. A platoon of bagpipers, playing Joni Mitchell's "River." Behind them was a trail of sidewalkers – not marching in formation but instead summoned to follow along, to see where this was going.

Sometimes you make plans. Sometimes plans make themselves.

Especially in New York City.

"Shall we?" I said, offering my hand. I was doing this to be romantic, and also because I was worried that my visual impairment was going to make it hard for me to march in a growing crowd.

"Let's," she replied, taking my hand to be romantic, and also because she was worried that my visual impairment was going to make it hard for me to march in a growing crowd.

Hand in hand, we headed down Second Avenue. It soon became very clear from the conversations of the people around us that nobody knew who the bagpipers were or where they were going. There were plenty of theories, though.

"I think it's the fire department's bagpipe corps," one older gentleman said.

"I'm not sure the NYFD plays Joni Mitchell," his companion replied. "She's Canadian, you know."

Meanwhile, the hipsters directly in front of us were in a bit of a lather.

"Do you think it's Where's Fluffy?" a skinny guy in a cardigan asked.

"It's not like Where's Fluffy to play in the daylight," a disheveled guy in a pea coat replied.

"Which is why it would be *so* Where's Fluffy! To fool us by playing in the daylight!" the skinny guy rebutted.

I wasn't sure what any of this meant. What I was sure of was that the bagpipes had begun to play "Fairytale of New York" – which is basically the best Christmas song ever written.

"Where do you think we're going?" Lily asked.

I knew it wasn't meant as an existential question. But that's how my mind chose to hear it. Maybe because I was still trying to loosen myself from my father and the mood of foreboding that he put me in. Maybe because I was still wondering if Lily and I had found safe ground again. Or maybe just because we were blindly following eleven bagpipers, and while not a single one of them appeared to be pied, I was sure caution needed to be exercised whenever random pipers were concerned.

More and more people joined us as we crossed through midtown. For one scary moment, I thought we were going to head to Times Square, which would have been a literal tourist trap at this point in the season. But instead we skirted around it, an accumulation of curiosities following a single tune.

By the time we got to Tompkins Square Park, there had to be at least two hundred of us. There was a pause in the music as the bagpipers assembled in the park's central circle. The hipsters peered around, looking for another band to show up. But the bagpipers were the only show around – and now they were ready for another song.

Even though it wasn't even noon, they started to play the opening strains of "Silent Night." Even though it wasn't night, we all fell silent, something in the sounds reaching far within us. Such a peaceful song, and so sad. Even though there weren't any words, we were all filling in the words in our heads.

All is calm, all is bright.

I didn't really believe in Christmas carols, but I could believe in them a little more if, like this, they pushed us a little closer to wonder, a little closer to gratitude. Even the hard years have some reason for celebration, and I was feeling it now, and hoping that Lily was feeling it, too.

The next song wasn't a Christmas song – it was Van Morrison's "Into the Mystic." Some people in the audience started to sing along. I could tell Lily had no idea what song it was, so I started to serenade her with my own off-key rendition, telling her we were born before the wind, also younger than the sun. Telling her that when that foghorn blows, I'd be coming home. Telling her I wanted to rock her gypsy soul.

She smiled at that, showing me some of that gypsy soul shining through.

By the last verse, she was singing along. Then even more so when they transitioned into a rousing rendition of Sam Cooke's "A Change is Gonna Come." We were all singing along now, joined by more and more people who were coming to the park and finding this strange, piper-drawn chorus. This spoke more to me than any 70-percent-off sale, more than any Hollywood construction, more than any check my father could write or any commercial that could be put on TV.

I put my arm around Lily's shoulder and she put her arm around my waist, and we stayed like that – two bodies, one entity – for the rest of the song. Then we moved our arms so we could applaud with the rest of the crowd. The eleven bagpipers bowed once to us, then once to each other, then disappeared into the day.

"I'm so glad we," Lily said.

"Yeah, I'm so glad we as well."

"I think it's time for a Salty Pimp, don't you?" Lily suggested.

I nodded enthusiastically, and we headed over to Big Gay Ice Cream for a Salty Pimp (vanilla ice cream, dulce de leche, sea salt, chocolate dip) and an American Globs (vanilla ice cream, pretzels, sea salt, chocolate dip). Then we headed over to Mercer Street to get some coffee at Think, where we were helped by a stupendous pink-haired barista who didn't flinch when I ordered an iced vanilla soy latte at the end of December. There was just enough time to stop off on Eighth Street to get Langston and Benny a Beyoncé-shaped lamp as a Christmas/housewarming gift.

("Why a lamp?" I asked Lily.

"New Jersey doesn't get as much light," she replied, still a little bitter, but not so bitter that she opted for a Mariah Carey lamp instead.)

By the time we were done shopping, my eye was starting to ache, and Lily was due to walk some dogs. We split up – but only temporarily. I went off to my apartment and rested, and then at night Lily came over with pizza and some holiday movies to watch. She was shocked that I'd never seen *Love Actually*, and I was shocked that it wasn't that bad, actually. And we may not have agreed upon whether *The Nightmare Before Christmas* was a Christmas movie or a Halloween movie, but we enjoyed it nonetheless.

At the end of the movie, we lay there for a few minutes, letting the TV screen fall silent and blue after the end credits.

"I like it like this," I said. "When we can just be ourselves. Give or take an eye patch."

Lily kissed my lips, kissed my eye patch, kissed the eyelid she could reach.

"I've got to go wrap some presents," she said. Then she reached into her bag and pulled out the red Moleskine.

"Instructions for tomorrow," she informed me.

I promised her I wouldn't open it until morning.

The minute she left the apartment, I missed having her there. But as with all loves, I supposed, the consolation was in the fact that she'd be back.

12
LILY

Pa Rum Pum Pum Pum Scum

Wednesday, December 24th

I didn't mean to leave my boyfriend stranded at the Strand on the most frantic shopping day of the year. I hadn't intended to strand him at each stop I'd planned for this day on this year's Moleskine adventure tour.

The night of The Great Glitterskating Massacre, after all the commotion, I was late tending to the walking needs of my roster of dogs with owners away for the holidays. I hadn't followed Dash to the emergency room because I knew he was in the safe (and bloodied – SO SORRY!) hands of many kind, wounded librarians. If those people could handle books so well, I knew they could handle Dash, despite my worry about not accompanying him to the hospital.

"Go," Dash said when I insisted I could tend to my dogs later, after he was stitched up and made better. "I'll be relieved not to worry about you worrying about your dogs who need to be relieved."

I didn't finish my dog-walking duties until late that night, and I was exhausted by the time I got home. I couldn't fall asleep until I came up with a plan to right the situation. Feeling guilty – and cheated of my original grand plan to celebrate Dash – I stayed awake creating a makeup-fun-day plan for Christmas Eve. I organized the day and wrote the instructions in the red Moleskine notebook.

Instead of further drowning in apologies for causing Dash's dear face to be maimed, I thought we could celebrate it. I was going to give him the best pirate day of his life. I was wrong.

Sorry.

10:00 a.m.

Yo ho ho
To Park Slope we go
We'll meet at the Superhero store
We'll scuttle a man-o'-war

Our first stop would be the Superhero Supply Co. store, with its secret back door leading to a room where the perils of after-school writing tutoring happened. As much as I loved my phone's new lock-screen photo of Dash as Santa, I couldn't wait to change it to Dash as full pirate, with legit-earned pirate patch over his eye, a tricorne hat, a swashbuckler's white frilly shirt, and the sea captain's galleon coat we could buy in the Superhero store. While we were there, we could inquire about putting in volunteer applications for literary goodness in the secret back room, which would be a much better celebration flourish than a glitter massacre. And good experience for my potential future librarian man.

The Moleskine directed Dash to meet me at the Superhero store at 11:30 a.m. on Christmas Eve day. Before I left for our adventure, I had to tend to Boris. My dog and I had spent the previous night at Mrs. Basil E.'s to visit with Grandpa, and I was about to take Boris for a quick morning walk around, and not in, Gramercy Park. He could do his business and I could think about all the presents I was going to unwrap tomorrow, and all the kisses I'd steal from my pirate boyfriend today.

I had Boris on the leash and was about to step outside Mrs. Basil E.'s townhouse for our loop around the park when I heard the refrains of a group of carolers performing outside the gated entrance to Gramercy Park. In faux hip-hop style, these middle-aged white guys were singing and beatboxing to the tune of "The Little Drummer Boy." A huge crowd was gathered around them, applauding and grooving to the beat. I recognized the performers, and prayed that Grandpa, still eating his breakfast in the back of the house, could not hear them.

Grandpa didn't hate the song. He hated the group.

They'd been a plague to the East Village and Lower East Side last year. They called themselves the Canarsie Crèche Crew, and they were a barbershop quartet of convicted Wall Street con men who'd met in prison and, once released, moved to South Brooklyn to resume their lives as bad guys. Now, instead of swindling investors, they performed for tourists while their non-singing member stole the tourists' wallets, iPhones, shopping bags, and other valuables.

I didn't close the front door to Mrs. Basil E.'s house fast enough. "NO!" I heard Grandpa shout from behind me in the hallway. He barreled outside with all the speed an octogenarian with a cane and a heart condition could muster. From the top of the stoop, he shook his cane in the direction of the singers and shouted, "Scum! You're scum! Police! Police!"

Grandpa's sudden appearance on the stoop was too hurried, causing the concerned Boris to bolt toward the street, his leash still attached to my hand, pulling me down the stairs with him. "Lily!" Grandpa cried out as I fell to the ground. I was totally fine, maybe I'd have a minor bruise or two, but Grandpa tried to reach down the steps to help me up.

He fell. Hard.

Mrs. Basil E. called 911. I called Dash.

11:30 a.m.
My call to Dash had gone straight to voice mail. He'd been stranded in Brooklyn on the F train (also known to locals as the "Fudge Me!" train, except not the word "fudge," because of its perpetual lateness). When he finally got above

ground again and texted me, I told him to meet me at the Moleskine's next destination so I could stay with Grandpa till he was discharged from the hospital.

I was too scared to deal with reality. I refused to see it.

After Grandpa was seen by the ER doctor, I sent an update to Dash. *Grandpa just needs to get bandaged. He'll be fine. I'll meet you at the next stop! I'm SO SORRY!*

Dash the Pirate texted back, *Aaargh! Can Santa feel his face? I mean, Grandpa?*

I laughed. The smile's release to my tense jaw felt so good.

Some bruises on his cheeks and a bump on his head, I typed back. *But he's already asking for lunch, so that means he's fine. And certainly he's feeling his stomach!*

Dash replied, *Take your time. I'm having a delightful morning scaring all the precocious children shoppers of Park Slope with my eye.*

You're showing them your eye patch?

No, I'm taking it off for them. Pause. *And now I've been asked to leave the store. See you soon!*

3:00 p.m.

On a Clipper City boat we'll scavenge,
In the Pirate's Booty bar we'll ravage
The Manhattan isle we'll go around

While I scream I LOVE YOU aloud
Ahoy, matey!

I totally lost track of time. And my cell signal was spotty. Why is cell service so bad in the places you need it most, like hospitals, the subway, the movies?

So many doctors came in and came out.

My parents arrived.

Great-Uncles Sal and Carmine arrived.

Benny and Langston and Cousin Mark arrived.

It was almost like a party in Grandpa's hospital room. My relatives were actually wrapping the presents in their shopping bags to pass the time. Or to not lose more time, since Christmas was tomorrow.

Grandpa had a room now. The doctors wanted to keep him under observation for a few hours.

No one said why.

I'd clipped our tickets to the page with the Moleskine directions for pirate destination number two.

I forgot to meet Dash there.

It's okay! Dash texted me. *There's nothing better for a wounded cornea than being wind-whipped across the Hudson River.*

Sorry.

Don't be. I just got offered a job slinging drinks in the Pirate's Booty bar.

Because you're wearing a pirate's patch?

No. Because I'm the only sober person down here.

6:00 p.m.

Shiver me timbers!
Back to the Strand we'll go
Aglow aglow aglow
We'll find books about hornswogglers, landlubbers, and
    scallywags
Locked back in the basement we'll contemplate a sh . . .

I didn't make it there either.

I typed: *Sorry! Again!*

Don't be sorry. Being stranded at the Strand during last-minute shopping chaos is actually the most relaxing place in the world to me. You really do love me!

You're interrogating people trying to sell their books back, aren't you?

No, I'm slumped in a chair in the We're Here, We're Queer section, about to take a nap. SO HAPPY. So don't apologize. How's Grandpa?

The cardiologist delivered the news while Grandpa slept. "I recommend he move to an assisted-living facility."

A polite way of saying Grandpa's most dreaded words: *nursing home.*

Mrs. Basil E. said, "Nonsense. He can live with me. I can provide the care he needs."

Dr. Jerkface asked, "Does your home have stairs?"

Mrs. Basil E. said, "It's a five-story townhouse. Of course it does."

Dr. Jerkface said, "He's at great risk if he falls again. Are you prepared to install chairlifts? Old Manhattan brownstones don't accommodate those well."

"I can convert the street-level rooms for him."

"Are you prepared to provide live-in nursing care? His anti-coagulant medication needs to be vigorously monitored. He can bruise easily, as you see on his face, and is at risk for mini-strokes. Stairs are the biggest danger to his condition. To say nothing of five levels of them."

Mom's face was grim but resigned. "We knew this day was coming. Do we face it now or stall again, only to be left with the same choice a few months or a year from now, and risk that his condition will have deteriorated more in the meantime?"

In my heart, I knew it was the best option for Grandpa. I just knew how much he'd hate it, how hard he'd resist it, and my heart squeezed in pain for him. The doctor's recommendation was meant to extend and improve Grandpa's quality of life. To Grandpa, it would be a death sentence.

I expected Mrs. Basil E. to argue with my mother, but instead she sighed and said, "You're right."

Great-Uncle Carmine asked, "Should we cancel this year's Christmas-night party?" A family tradition going on fifty years. Sacrilege! To cancel it was a sure sign of the end of the world.

"No," said Mrs. Basil E. "The party is still on. Now, more than ever, we must celebrate."

That's when I lost it.

7:00 p.m.

They didn't call it that, but I was basically put in a tantrum room. It was a discreet comfort area, with white padded walls and soft chairs and no other hard objects, where patients' grieving loved ones were taken so they could lose their shit. Yes, I said it. SHIT.

This situation was shit.

Christmas was shit.

Everything was shit.

Mrs. Basil E. accompanied me. She was always the only person besides Grandpa who could calm me down, even though she'd been the one to cause my meltdown to begin with, by suggesting we *celebrate* during this dark holiday.

I shrieked. I screamed. I begged. "Please don't make him go to the old people's home! You know he always says the only way he's leaving his family is in a box."

Mrs. Basil E. said nothing.

"Say something!" I demanded.

She said nothing.

"Please," I said quietly. Sincerely.

"This hurts me as much as it will hurt him," she finally said. "But the family has convened, and everyone is in agreement. The time has come."

"Grandpa won't be in agreement."

"You don't know Grandpa as well as you think. He can

be irascible, but he also wants what's best for his family. He doesn't want to be a burden."

"He's not a burden! How could you say such a thing?"

"I agree. He's *not* a burden. It's a *privilege* to walk through this life with him as my big brother. But as his condition continues to deteriorate, he will feel like a burden. It already weighs heavily on his heart, which is why he'd wanted to move to my house to begin with. He's known this day was coming, despite his resistance."

I felt so stupid, and selfish, and irresponsible. Grandpa was doomed to a nursing home – his worst fear. Since his heart attack, I'd doted on him, cared for him, practically stopped my life to help him avoid this outcome. For what?

And I'd spent our last holiday season together before he was confined to a home goofing off with my wonderful boyfriend.

My wonderful boyfriend! Whom I'd led on a wild goose chase all day!

I cried. And Mrs. Basil E. let me, without pulling me to her for comfort.

"Let it out," was all she said.

"Why aren't you crying, too?" I asked her between sniffles.

"Because this is only going to get worse," she said. "So we must buck up, put on a kind face, and get on with it."

"Get on with what?"

"Life. In all its bittersweet glory."

9:00 p.m.

A miracle finally happened.

Snow. It wasn't a major storm but a light, soft, sweet dusting. As I strolled alone back to Mrs. Basil E.'s so I could walk my dog and feed Grandpa's cat, then tend to my client dogs before returning to the hospital, the feel of the snow warmed my cold heart. I stuck my tongue out to taste it. Bittersweet, indeed. And a welcome sign of normalcy. But it was the night before the usually most exciting day of the year. Nothing was right. Nothing was normal.

Dash was sitting on Mrs. Basil E.'s stoop when I arrived. Dash! My phone battery had died an hour ago and I'd given up trying to communicate more apologies to him.

He was wearing a tricorne pirate's hat. Snowflakes dotted his eye patch. Boris sat next to him. I'd never seen a more handsome sight.

"Aaargh," Dash said, and pulled me to his chest. "Boris has been walked and Grunt has been fed," he whispered in my ear. "And your client list taken care of for tonight."

Sorry, I didn't say.

"I love you so much," I did say.

We didn't say more. We just held on. He stroked my hair as I lay my head on his chest, now cloaked in a new galleon coat.

I could feel the ridges of a book pressing through his coat pocket, and I knew it was the Moleskine that had led him on the day's hollow quests. Of all the people last Christmas who could have found the red notebook peeking through the other millions (and miles) of books in the Strand, Dash had been the one to find it for a reason. I don't know what will happen between him and me in the future, and I hope I'll be okay with whatever does, but I know that no matter what, he was drawn to that notebook because he belongs with us.

He's family.

13
DASH

And So This Is Christmas...

Thursday, December 25th

Boomer was bummed.

Sofia's family had insisted on spending Christmas in Spain, so he was solo again. Forlorn, he came over to my mother's apartment so we could head to Mrs. Basil E.'s party together.

"Don't worry," I told him as I locked up and we sallied forth. "It'll be over in a blink."

"A blink is a very short amount of time," Boomer replied. Then he demonstrated a blink. "See?"

I was about to tell him I was accustomed to the general duration of a blink, but then he continued.

"But I guess a blink is a good thing, right? Because if you didn't do it, you'd be staring all the time. And your eyes would hurt. So maybe a blink is okay, if you're saying it metaphysically."

"I think you mean metaphorically," I corrected.

"No," Boomer said, perfectly serious. "I mean

metaphysically. Everything is the way it is. You blink. Then you're back, and everything is the way it was ... except that parts of it have to be a little different. But that blink? Completely necessary."

I thought about this the rest of the way – maybe Lily and I had just been through a blink. Maybe our eyes were back open. (Or at least one of my eyes was back open ... but that was more a medical thing than a metaphorical or metaphysical one.)

I was lugging Lily's Christmas present – I had ordered her the finest cookie sheets to be found on the Internet and had also used my father's Christmas check (mailed to my mother's house) to get her baking lessons at the French Culinary Institute, downtown.

I'd tied the cookie sheets with a bow instead of wrapping them, so I wasn't that surprised when Boomer said, "I think it's so cool that you got Lily those little sleds. They'll be awesome when it snows. We'll have to go to the park!"

"And what did you get Sofia?" I asked.

"I know when she gets back she's going to miss home, so I got all of these photos of Barcelona off the Internet and put them in one of those digital frames, and then also got one of those projectors, so if she wants to be in her room and think she's back in Barcelona, she should be able to do that."

I tried to remember the last present I'd bought Sofia – I think it had been a Gund teddy bear. Lily was the first girlfriend I'd ever had who I'd given presents that weren't

216

purchased (sardonically or not) in a toy store.

"How did you get good at this whole dating thing?" I asked Boomer. Part of me couldn't believe I was asking him this. But a bigger part of me really wanted to know.

"I don't think I'm good at it," Boomer told me. "But when I'm with Sofia I'm not really thinking about whether or not I'm good at it, which is what makes it good. Then I go home and worry. But then I'm back with her and it's good again. I think that's what dating is."

Mrs. Basil E.'s joint was already jumping when we got there – I recognized some of the people, and a good number I didn't. I waved to the librarians, who raised their glasses in salute. Since I didn't want to saddle Lily with the cookie sheets straightaway, I hid them behind a statue of Dame Judi Dench.

Boomer spotted Yohnny and bounced over to him to say hi. I looked for Lily, but couldn't find her in the parlor or the drawing room.

I felt a little silly going up to Mrs. Basil E. and asking, "Have you seen my girlfriend?" Luckily, I didn't have to ask.

"If you are searching for She Who Shall Not Be Called Lily Bear But Shall Remain Lily Bear In Our Stubborn Loving Hearts, she is in the kitchen with my brother. Please tell them to get out and mingle. A party, like the human body, will fall into rigor mortis without proper circulation."

I headed to the kitchen. I was a little worried about what Grandpa would look like, after what Lily had told me about yesterday. It was a relief to see that even though he stayed seated rather than jump up to shake my hand, the gleam in his eye was still very much present when he saw me walk in.

"If it isn't Long Dash Silver!" he laughed. "She told me it was bad . . . but, wow, you look like you lost a fight with an octopus. I hope you at least got a few shots in."

"I got at least four of its arms. How are you feeling?"

"Fit as a fiddle! Granted, it's a fiddle that's been played for eighty-four years straight. But still making music!" Slowly, but resolutely, he got up from his chair. "Now I'm going to leave you two to catch up. I know Inga's out there somewhere serving the canapés, and I'd go all the way out to Canarsie for one of her canapés."

It wasn't until Grandpa had shuffled out of the room that Lily said, "It makes me so sad."

"I know," I told her. "But if it makes his life better, and he's okay with it, then your sadness is kinda beside the point."

Lily recoiled at that, and her recoil made me realize how awful what I said had sounded.

I quickly jumped back in. "What I mean is . . . he and Mrs. Basil E. are very smart people. They know what they're doing."

Lily was still irate. "Are you saying I don't know what I'm doing?"

"Agh! No!"

Lily was out of her own chair now. "Just LET ME BE SAD. Why can't anyone *let me be sad*?!"

I answered carefully. "Lily, you don't need anyone to let

you be sad. Be sad. Be happy. Be thrilled. Be despondent. But don't lose sight of everyone else. Not when you're happy, and not when you're sad."

"Well, I'm sorry if you feel I've been *ignoring you* –"

"No!"

"You don't get it. Nobody's going to live in my house anymore, Dash. Nobody!"

"But they're all going to be living *somewhere*. They're all going to be near."

"I know. But . . ." Lily trailed off.

I tried to pick up the trail. "But?"

"But *I don't like it*, okay? I don't like how everything is changing. It's like when you're a kid, you think that things like the holidays are meant to show you how things always stay the same, how you have the same celebration year after year, and that's why it's so special. But the older you get, the more you realize that, yes, there are all these things that link you to the past, and you're using the same words and singing the same songs that have always been there for you, but each time, things have shifted, and you have to deal with that shift. Because maybe you don't notice it every single day. Maybe it's only on days like today that you notice it a lot. And I know I'm supposed to be able to deal with that, but I'm not sure I can deal with that. Like us, Dash. Look at us. I mean, at first when we were together, it was like there wasn't such a thing as time, right? We were so much in the present that it was never going to be any different – it was all about finding out, and not so much about knowing. It was all so intense and all so immediate, and I think maybe I thought, okay, this is what having a boyfriend I really like is all about. And then, this is what having a boyfriend I love is all about. But then time comes into it, and it's not as immediate, and it's not as intense, and you can't help but feel that something's getting lost there, right? The same as when someone moves away. Or isn't around anymore. Maybe you're okay with that something being lost, Dash. Maybe you don't care. But I care, Dash. I care a lot. Because I feel it a lot. And I don't have any idea what to do about it."

"Neither do I!" I confessed. "I have been trying for months to figure out a way to make it better, Lily. And the only answer I can come up with is to tell you there are some things you can't control, and time is, like, number one on that list. Number two is the actions of other people. I watched my father destroy my mother – absolutely destroy her. And then I watched them both destroy their marriage and the entity that was the only thing I'd ever known as *family*. I know I was only eight, but even if I'd been eighteen, there wouldn't have been anything I could do but protect myself. I wanted to do anything I could, but the answer was to realize that it was not something that I got to decide. Even now. I cannot change my father. And I want to, so badly. I will even admit to you now that one of the reasons I want to change my father is because I feel that if I can change everything that's wrong with him, then maybe I can change all those parts in me, too. Isn't that scary? But isn't it also natural, to want that?"

"You never told me that."

"I know! But I'm telling you now – I'm telling you all of this now – because I know there are all of these things happening to you where what you feel is, as I said before in the wrong way, beside the point. You can't stop time. You can't make everyone healthy or always in love. You can't. But you and me – what we have – that's one thing we *do* have control over. That's the one thing that's up to us. There are times when it feels to me like it's all up to you. And I'm sure there are times for you when it feels like it's all up to me. But we have to move forward like it's up to *us,* together. I know it's not as intense or immediate as it used to be – but that just means that instead of having only a present together, we're having a past, present, and future all at once."

Lily softened then. I could see it. She wasn't giving up. She wasn't giving in, per se. But she was understanding. I was feeling the same way. How had we never had this conversation before?

Probably because we hadn't been ready for this conversation before.

"It's not fair," Lily said, walking over to me and leaning in. "What's the one thing we want when it comes to the people we love? Time. And what's the scariest thing about how love goes? Time. The thing we want the most is the thing we fear the most, I guess. Time is going to run out. But in the meantime we have . . . everything."

She hugged me then, and I hugged her back, and we probably would have stayed like that for a very long time if Inga the caterer hadn't come in at that moment.

"I promise I wasn't listening," she said, which pretty much guaranteed she'd been listening. "I just need to get the cheese puffs out of the oven before they become cheese puffeds."

As we walked back down the hall to the party, I explained Boomer's Theory of the Blink to Lily. She liked it.

"We had our blink," she said.

"Yup."

"And now our eyes are open."

"Or eye."

"Or eye."

"And inevitably –"

"We'll blink again."

"But that's okay."

"Because things will be clearer after we do."

"Precisely."

We got to the door of the party. Friends, family, and strangers spread before us. There was a music to their conversation – this strange orchestration of good company.

I reached for her hand. She took mine.

"Let's do this," I said. "All of it."

14
LILY

The Present of Lily Present

Thursday, December 25th

It was an odd feeling – still so much sadness to process, and yet this felt like the best Christmas of my life.

All my favorite people gathered in my favorite house on my favorite day of the year. Laughing. Talking. Gifting. Eating. Nogging.

And Edgar Thibaud in a corner, the head of a group sitting in a circle around him, dealing a deck of cards to rapt elementary school-age party attendees, teaching them how to play poker.

"You invited Edgar Thibaud here?" Dash asked me.

"Grandpa did."

Actually, what Grandpa had said was, "You didn't invite Edgar Thibaud, did you? That woefully neglected hooligan high-fived me at the senior center and said he'd see me at my sister's Christmas party, and we could gather round the hearth and share a flask of hooch with some hoochie mamas."

I shuddered, recalling my Grandpa repeating Edgar's vulgar words. But I couldn't sustain the lie for more than a second. I amended my statement to Dash. "I mean, *I* did. Grandpa feels sorry for Edgar. He has no one at Christmas."

"For a reason."

"We must open our hearts to the downtrodden, and to scoundrels," I told Dash, and gave his hand a gentle squeeze. "'Tis the season."

"Edgar doesn't get a copy of the List, does he?"

I started to sputter, "Nnnooo," but Dash brushed my response away. He leaned in to me and whispered, "Should I be worried about your fascination with Edgar Thibaud? You don't look at that preposterous buffoon and wonder what it would be like to kiss him, do you?" Dash's one visible eyebrow was raised, about to the height of the eye patch on his other side, and his lips had a vague half-turn to them. He was teasing me.

"I do wonder," I confessed. "In the same way I wonder what it would be like to make out with an orangutan just before it has diarrhea."

"Thanks, now I lost my appetite for Inga's canapés."

I placed a kiss on his lips. "Is that better?"

"Delicious," said Dash. "Gingerbread-y."

My boyfriend really knew the words to excite me. I felt I should give the man who loves language a word gift in exchange. "Edgar's a *sycophantile.*"

"What?" Dash laughed.

"Someone who likes to surround himself with people

who will fawn all over him. He pays them to do that, you know. The chess players in the park. The Korean party kids. Probably those little second-grade hustlers on the floor there."

"Edgar pays people to hang out with him?"

"Yup. He has a roll of fivers in his argyle pockets at all times for just that purpose."

"It all makes sense now," said Dash.

Mrs. Basil E. stood on top of an ottoman and clinked her champagne glass. "Attention, my dear friends!" she called out. Usually at a party with that many people and that much nog in circulation, it takes more than one pronouncement to hush a room, but Mrs. Basil E. commanded that reaction immediately. She continued. "First, thank you for coming tonight. And Merry Christmas!"

"Happy Kwanzaa, Mrs. Oregano!" Boomer called back.

Mrs. Basil E. nodded at Boomer. "Thank you, Ricochet." She moved her eyes around the room to direct the crowd, landing her gaze on Grandpa, sitting by her side. "As you may know, we've had our share of challenges this year, and next year will bring a new set. So we are thankful now, for your friendship, to celebrate with you, to –"

Grandpa nudged her ankle with his cane. "Let me talk already!"

Mrs. Basil E. stepped down from the ottoman. "You don't have to be a Sadie about it," she chided him.

Grandpa smiled and stood up. He said, "It's a tradition going back many years that in the later hours of this

Christmas party, when the adults turn to singing –"

"And singing and singing and singing," his many nieces and nephews chimed in.

Grandpa continued, "Yes, and more singing, and the younger ones are exhausted and ready to go home to bed, that the grown-ups buy extra time for ourselves by putting a movie on in the basement for the kids to watch, and fall asleep to."

"*Wizard of Oz!*" said Kerry-cousin.

"*The Sound of Music!*" said Cousin Mark.

"*Make the Yuletide Gay!*" cried out Langston.

"What's that?" said Mrs. Basil E., looking scandalized – a Christmas movie she'd never heard of!

"Kidding," said Langston. "That was the after-after party. For those of us who could stay awake that late."

"Well, this year we have a special surprise," said Grandpa. His gaze fell fondly on me. "Lily, if you'll accompany me downstairs, my Christmas present for you is there. Those of you who want to watch a movie, please join us. Those of you who don't, don't! Continue making merry up here." He looked at Edgar Thibaud and shook his cane at him. "Any gambling wins tonight will be donated to the center."

Edgar laughed. I don't think he'd ever been ordered what to do by anyone besides a judge. The appalled stares from many partygoers let Edgar Thibaud know that Grandpa had not been joking. Edgar shrugged and said, "Okay, fair enough." A Christmas miracle! Generosity!

Some cousins started to head into the basement as Dash and I went to either side of Grandpa to lead him toward the stairs, and then help him down. "Did you know about this?" I asked Dash. It seemed weird to interrupt the party so early with a movie. I hoped it was an old home movie converted to DVD of Grandpa and his siblings as little ones.

"It's all been a grand conspiracy," said Dash.

When we reached the basement apartment, which Mrs. Basil E. kept as a man cave for family members during football and soccer seasons, with a proper bar and enormous television (she didn't allow TVs in any other room in the house), the TV was already on, with a blank screen. The bar was set up like a movie concession stand, with a popcorn maker and a glass display case of candies like M&M's, Milk Duds, Junior Mints, and an entire shelf with my favorites – Sno-Caps – tiered in the shape of a Christmas tree.

If I had any doubt what we were about to watch, it was removed when the blanket covering a life-size cardboard cutout next to the TV was removed. It was Helen Mirren as frail, elderly Bess, wearing a silk head scarf tied under her chin, and holding her movie corgi, Scrumpet!

"WHAT?" I shrieked, with all the decibel power of a tween girl getting a personal concert by the world's biggest boy band.

"Down, Shrilly!" Langston called out from somewhere inside the crowd of people.

My heart was beating so fast, I thought I might die of happiness. "How?" I asked Grandpa.

He said, "My friend whom you know as Mr. Panavision gets these lovely little doodads called screeners, because he's an awards-season voting guild member. He helped me get the screener and the promotional cutout. But Mr. Panavision has let me know that this is precious intellectual property, and the FBI will be called if the screener winds up in the hands of criminals, *so no one give it to Edgar Thibaud or let him down here.*"

Mom said, "The movie concession stand is from us, sweetie."

Dash said, "I arranged the Sno-Caps."

Langston said, "Poorly. It looks more like a poo pile."

For everything that was wrong in the world – war, global warming, Grandpa having to move to a nursing home, my lifelong family home being dismantled and probably sold – there was so much that was so right. My brother and my boyfriend bicker-bantering. My dad eating most of the Reese's Pieces before the other guests could get to them. Mrs. Basil E. holding court over a sea of guests. The smell of popcorn. My Grandpa hugging me. All the people I loved most gathered in one room, to watch a queen and her dog.

I'd thought my dream date would be sharing this movie alone in a movie theater with Dash. This cave was so much better. These people were my coven. Merry Christmas, Lily. Your Highness.

I loved the movie. I loved the party.

But, priorities.

Eighty-seven screen minutes of that precious nugget Scrumpet, and I needed to be reunited with my dog, *immediately*.

Certainly Boris's behavior had improved over the last year – he was down to maybe one or two pinning-a-human-to-the-floors per month, but he was not yet socialized to big parties, so he'd been left at my apartment during the Christmas party. So Dash and I took an early leave of Mrs. Basil E.'s after the movie so we could walk him and I could smother my face in his beastly fur.

After we walked him and I cried, telling Boris how much I loved him and would be honored to get lost in the deep forest surrounding Balmoral Castle with him, Dash and I returned to the apartment so I could give my boyfriend and my dog their Christmas presents. First I gave Boris a chew toy that he massacred within a minute of receiving. One moment it was a perfectly good Donald Trump doll. The next it was a flying toupee and dismembered body parts.

"That was beautiful, Boris," Dash told him, patting the satisfied dog's head. Then Dash crouched down to face Boris on Boris's level. Using his most queenly Helen Mirren voice to intone *Corgi & Bess*'s catch phrase, Dash reminded Boris: "'Always chew with dignity, dear Scrum.'"

My Christmas present to Dash was possibly going to make me lose my own dignity, but I tried to muster the courage to go through with it. Before I did, I gave him the easy part of his gift. We sat down next to Oscar, and I handed Dash his first present from under the tree. (Stealing a kiss – or five – from Dash meanwhile.)

I took the Santa hat I'd bought with Dash's $12.21 Macy's gift card, and placed it on his head. "Guess," I said.

Santa Dash held up the present and shook it. "Salt shaker?" he asked. It was clearly the size and shape of a book. "That Snuggie you knew Santa asked himself for? Because Santa doesn't have enough soft, warm things in his life already?" He looked down at Boris. "I'm not talking about you, softy. I'm partial to Prancer, as you know. No offense."

Boris licked Dash's ankle. No offense taken.

"Open it," I said.

Dash carefully removed the gift wrap and placed it to his side to reuse it. My eco-conscious dreamboat. "It's a book!" Dash cried out, with all the excitement of having been given a new car. "I don't believe it."

Then he took a closer look at the book – *A Christmas Carol*, but not just any edition. This one was red cloth with a blind-stamped binding and gilt lettering, design, and edges. "Lily! This isn't a first edition, is it?"

"I wish! I wanted to get you one, but that costs about thirty thousand dollars, and Mrs. Basil E. said if I wanted to continue on my mogul trajectory, I should be more frugal. So this is an exact replica of the 1843 first edition. Not the real deal. But less dusty and probably less a candidate to be a carrier of a century and a half's germs. And much more reasonably priced."

Dash clutched the book to his chest. "I love it!"

I leaned over to place a light kiss on his eye patch. And then I handed him another present. "This one was an impulse buy at the Strand. Rare book room."

He opened the second present. "*Treasure Island!*" he exclaimed.

"Bona fide first edition, with illustrations," I said proudly. "For my favorite pirate."

"*Aargh!*" exclaimed my pirate.

"There's more," I said.

"I can never get too many books!"

"Not books. The other present is something ... you have to see."

Here's where I needed my courage. And the hope he would have the dignity not to laugh when I made myself my most vulnerable and possibly the dorkiest I'd ever been – no small challenge.

Dash waited outside my bedroom while I changed privately. Then I half opened the door and invoked some words from one of his gift books. "Come in and know me better, man!"

Dash laughed, recognizing the quote from *A Christmas Carol*, and cautiously stepped inside. "Why all the secrecy?" he said.

I took a deep breath, and did it. I opened the door all the way, so he could see.

He had a sharp intake of breath – not of disgust, but surprise.

"You're the present of Lily present!" he said.

He got it! *Ding, ding, ding!*

It wasn't fancy lingerie, but it felt just as risky. I wore bright red undergarments ordered online from an old-fashioned ladieswear emporium: traditional Victorian bloomers – like loose capri pants with crocheted lace patterns below the knee, a tie-string waist, and a modest red corset covering my chest. By modern standards, I was overdressed. By Lily standards, I was practically naked. I didn't even have my glasses on.

"Think Mrs. Cratchit looked like this under her frock?" I asked Dash bashfully. Why was I standing so far from the light switch? I wanted to turn out the light immediately!

"Mrs. Fezziwig is more like it. She threw great parties. Just like you."

"She also maimed librarians?"

"Only when M-Fezz went ice-skating."

There was an awkward pause. I had the outfit. Now what were we supposed to do with it?

"Get over here, Lily Present," said Dash.

My pirate pulled me to him. He kissed me. And kissed me and kissed me and kissed me. Slowly. Deeply. Commandingly.

He stepped all the way inside my bedroom, and I tore Dash's Santa hat off his head, running my hands across his hair, placing more kisses on his forehead, his cheeks, his beautiful lips. "Santa can definitely feel his face," Dash muttered.

Then we heard my parents stumble into the foyer, tipsy and laughing.

"Should we check on her?" my dad asked.

"You know she falls asleep before midnight every Christmas," said Mom. "Can never stay awake after all the excitement of the day."

We heard them stumble toward their bedroom door.

I moved toward my own bedroom door, assuming Dash would conclude our make-out session and return to his own home now that my parents were here.

Instead Dash said, "Close the door, Lily."

The door stayed closed less than one minute before it opened again, with no knock to precede it.

Dad tossed Dash's tricorne hat into the room and said, "Good night, Jack Sparrow."

Dash said, "I take Depp offense."

"Good," said Dad. "Now go home."

I walked Dash to the foyer and kissed him good night.

"Know what the best thing your true love can give you is?" I asked him.

"What?" said Dash.

"True love."

He kissed me one last time, placed his pirate hat on his head, winked his non-patched eye at me, and took off.

I was not tired at all, and I had those beautiful new cookie sheets Dash had given me. Time to start baking.

Only 364 days left until next Christmas!

Thank you as always to our family and friends.

Thank you to Jennifer Rudolph Walsh, Bill Clegg, Alicia Gordon, and everyone at WME and The Clegg Agency.

Thank you for Nancy Hinkel, as always, for making being edited feel like a holiday. Thank you to the many, many people at Random House Children's Books who have made our books such a wonderful home, including (but in no way limited to) Stephen Brown, Jennifer Brown, Melanie Cecka, Barbara Marcus, Mary McCue, Adrienne Waintraub, Laura Antonacci, and Lisa Nadel. And thank you to Egmont, Text, and all our foreign publishers for their ace support.

Finally, thanks to everyone who told us how much Dash and Lily has meant to them over the years. This book wouldn't exist without you.